EASY READ

The Economist

丁一 著

《經濟學人》這樣讀就對了！

五南圖書出版公司 印行

序

　　國人從小學就開始英文的學習過程，中學、高中和大學皆有英文的必修課程。學測、基測、升等考試和各項公職考試皆有考英文，一般學生更是將英文單字和英文文法背得滾瓜爛熟。但是一般人對於英文文章的閱讀卻是頭痛異常，查遍整篇英文單字、熟悉英文文法，但是仍然無法明瞭整篇英文文章的內容，問題出在那裡？

　　筆者認為可能與我們對英文的學習態度有關，如果我們仍然停留在英文只是考試科目的話，英文當然無法進步，如果把英文當作是閱讀外國文章或是新聞雜誌（週刊）的工具，我們的英文程度就能大幅進步。我們每天接觸世界著名的英文新聞週刊相當多，包括《時代雜誌》（*Time*）、《新聞週刊》（*Newsweek*）、《商業週刊》（*Businessweek*）和英國的《經濟學人》（*The Economist*），筆者首選為《經濟學人》。

　　已有百年歷史的《經濟學人》，成立於 1843 年，旗下擁有英文《金融時報》（*Financial Times*）和教科書出版集團皮爾生出版社（Pearson PLC.），與商業金融資訊服務公司《經濟資訊新報》（*Economist Intelligence Unit*），皆是全球金融業、企業界和大專院校必須訂閱的重量級刊物。有別於一般性的新聞週刊，每週出版的《經濟學人》報導內容涵蓋全球各國最新的政經發展，立論精闢的企業策略發展分析文章、金融業最新發展趨勢、學術論文研討會文摘評論、公正不阿的書評文章、科技新知報導和墓誌銘，都是令人一讀再讀回味無窮的文章。為了增加週刊閱讀的多樣性，《經濟學人》的訂閱戶還能免費下載週刊全文朗讀版的 MP3 檔和全文電子書檔，方便讀者能隨時隨地的閱讀《經濟學人》。而不定期出版的針對國家發展、產業趨勢，以及社會議題的特刊報導，更是各國政要、專業人士和其他新聞媒體閱讀和轉載的材料。這些文章中的英文用字遣詞精簡，卻又呈現了英文寫作的功力，如果想要透過閱讀提升英文閱讀和寫作實力的話，同時增廣國際視野，我的選擇就是《經濟學人》。

筆者訂閱《經濟學人》二十年，深切體認閱讀這本週刊的好處無窮，想要把這本週刊介紹給國人。但是首先必須要有閱讀這本週刊的方法，因此野人獻曝，以簡單的英文文法編寫《經濟學人這樣讀就對了》這本工具書，書中以國中程度的英文文法，配合《經濟學人》的文章寫作例句方式做介紹，能幫助國人事半功倍，大幅提升英文閱讀能力，增廣國際視野。希望在閱讀本工具書之後，配合習題演練，能讓讀者皆能輕易的閱讀英文新聞文章。筆者才疏學淺編寫此書，匆促之餘若有筆誤，歡迎讀者來函不吝指教，請 mail 至 ylliaw@yahoo.com.tw，以便再版時做更正，本書另有教學 PPT 軟體和測驗題庫，歡迎教師來函索取，謝謝。

丁一

本 書 特 點

　　本書針對國際權威雜誌《經濟學人》（週刊）（*The Economist*）的寫作方式與英文句型結構，以簡單文法，配合工具書編排方式，協助讀者在閱讀本書後，能以輕鬆的能力閱讀《經濟學人》雜誌，增加國際視野，提升英文閱讀能力，全書共九章分別為：

1. **單字詞性**→說明英文單字詞性在句子中的擺放位置問題，奠定英文閱讀和作文基礎。

2. **句子結構**→說明《經濟學人》常用的四大句型，簡單句、複合句、複雜句和複合複雜句，明瞭寫作句型。

3. **子句**→三大子句：形容詞子句、名詞子句和副詞子句，分析句型變化原則。

4. **分詞、分詞片語和分詞構句**→《經濟學人》文章最常用的分詞用法，延伸句型的寫作方法。

5. **動名詞和動名詞片語**→動詞的延伸，增加英文閱讀能力。

6. **直接引用句和間接引用句**→《經濟學人》對新聞事件之最常用的寫作方法。

7. **數字的閱讀**→《經濟學人》文章中對數字的各種寫法。

8. **圖表的閱讀**→文章中圖表和統計數字的閱讀。

9. **其他**→其他附加的英文寫作方式。

　　各章內容包括（1）例句解說、（2）英文例句中譯、（3）句型結構、（4）例句練習、（5）綜合練習、（6）解答和（7）單字表。

　　本書適合大專院校開設下列課程「新聞英文」、「英文翻譯」和「商用英文」之教科書或個人自修英文閱讀工具書之用。

目錄

▸▸CONTENTS 目錄

目錄

第一章 單字詞性

導論

　　要能閱讀《經濟學人》並且徹底了解每一句其中的涵義,最基本的方法為了解英文單字的詞性,才不會造成每一句的單字皆查完字典後加上註解,但是合成一句還是不懂其中的意思。學習英文的困難度在於相同的英文單字,放在句中不同的位置就有不同的意義,其中的關鍵就是英文單字在不同的地方有不同的詞性,也有不同的意義,例如,book 的例句如下:

1. This is a book. 這是一本書。

　　book 在這裡是名詞(n)——單字意義是書。

2. Mary says "Book it." 瑪麗說「預訂」。

　　Book 在這裡是動詞(v)——單字意義是預訂(預約)。

3. There is a booking office at the corner.

　　轉角處有一個簽注站(售票處)。

　　booking 在這裡是分詞(Ving),當作形容詞來形容後面的 office 名詞。

4. Booking 預訂

　　booking 在這裡是動名詞(G)——單字意義是預訂。

　　從上面的例句分析可知,book 在不同的句子中的不同位置上,就有不同的意義。

　　要了解英文單字的字義變化最好的方式,就是重新了解英文單字的詞性。

　　英文單字的詞性可分為八大詞類:名詞(n)、代名詞(pron)、形容詞(adj)、動詞(v)、副詞(adv)、介系詞(prep)、連接詞(conj)和感嘆詞(Int),這些單字詞性在英文句子中有其固定的位置,詳細說明如下:

■1.1 名詞

在簡單句（主詞＋動詞＋受詞；S＋V＋O）的架構下，名詞擺在句首當主詞和擺在句尾當受詞。例如：

Mary Lin is a girl.
　　　S　　*V*　　*O*

林瑪麗是一位女孩。

在例句中 Mary Lin 是名詞，當本句中的主詞，而 girl 是名詞，當本句中的受詞。一般來說，英文句子大都以名詞當主詞，而其結尾也是以名詞當作受詞做結束。有時也以專有名詞當作主詞做句子的主詞或受詞，例如：

The University of Washington is a famous university.
　　　　　　S　　　　　　　　　*V*　　　　*O*

華盛頓大學是一所有名的大學。

在例句中，專有名詞 The University of Washington 在句子中當作主詞來使用。

Mary is going to the United States of America.
　S　　*V*　　　　　　*O*

在例句中，專有名詞 the United States of America 在句子中當作受詞來使用。

🖋 1-1 練習

▶ 請將下列句中的名詞找出來。

1. The hard work is starting now.
2. The economy was growing strongly in 2010s.
3. Brazil's president Lula is preparing to hand oved power to his successor.
4. "What kind of government would he run?" Mary said.
5. It is the dawn of nuclear age.
6. Frank Lin is working at Google in Mountain View headquarters.
7. Wealth management and asset management were the expertise of Lehman Brothers.
8. China is expected to take over Japan as the world's second largest economy.
9. The United States and Japan had held join military exercise at the Yellow Sea.
10. The growth engine of world economy will come from emerging nations in the next decade.

📖 1-1 解答

1. *the hard work*
   中譯:艱苦的工作剛開始。
2. *the economy*
   中譯:在 2010 年代經濟快速的成長。
3. *Brazil's president Lula*
   中譯:巴西總統魯拉準備交棒給他的接班人。
4. *Mary*
   中譯:瑪麗說:「他如何治理這個國家?」
5. *the dawn of nuclear age*
   中譯:核能時代來臨了。
6. *Frank Lin, Google in Mountain View headquarters*
   中譯:法蘭克林於 Google 位在 Mountain View 的總公司工作。

7. *Wealth management and asset management, the expertise of Lehman Brothers*

中譯:財富管理和資產管理是雷曼兄弟的專長。

8. *China, Japan, the world's second largest economy*

中譯:中國在不久的將來將取代日本成為世界第二大經濟體。

9. *The United States and Japan, join military exercise, at the Yellow Sea*

中譯:美國和日本在黃海展開聯合軍事演習。

10. *The growth engine of world economy, emerging nations in the next decade*

中譯:下個世紀世界經濟的成長將由新興國家所主導。

■1.2 代名詞

　　代名詞顧名思義就是代替「第一次」出現的名詞，在第二次出現時句子中的主詞和受詞的位置。例如：

She is waiting her mother at the railroad station.
pron
她在車站等待母親。

　　這個句中文法完全正確，但是文意卻不通，因為讀者不曉得"She"代表誰。如果把上句改寫如下便完全正確了：

Mary Lin is a girl. She is waiting her mother at the station.
　　　　　　　　　pron
林瑪麗是一位女孩。她在車站等待母親。

　　在例句中，我們知道"She"代名詞就是代表上一句中的林瑪麗。再看下一個例句：

A monkey was run over by a car. Mary Lin took it to the
　　　　　　　　　　　　　　　　　　　　　pron
veterinary hospital for treatment.
有一隻猴子被車子輾過。林瑪麗將牠帶到獸醫院治療。

　　在例句中，我們知道 it 代名詞就是代表上一句中的 a monkey。代名詞一定要在名詞先行詞出現之後才能在下一句出現，這樣才能夠清楚的代替名詞，不會造成讀者在閱讀上的混淆。

　　代名詞的延伸就是關係代名詞，例如 who, which, when 和 that 等，以上這些稱之為關係代名詞，因為大都為用在形容詞子句中，和其前面的先行名詞有關係，例如 who 代替人、which 代替物、when 代替時間、that 代替人和物。例句如下：

1. Mary Lin who is 19 years old is a girl.
　　19歲的林瑪麗是一位女孩。

2. The bike which was stolen was found by the police.
　　失竊的那輛腳踏車被警方找到了。

3. **The date when Mary Lin is available is marked for staff meeting.**

林瑪麗有空閒的日子，已經安排好作為員工會議時間。

4. **I saw Mary Lin and her dog that were running along the street.**

我看見林瑪麗和她的狗沿著馬路跑。

代名詞若依照它在句子結構中當主詞和受詞的角色，又可分為主格、所有格和受格，其用法列表如表 1-1。

表1-1	代名詞的格		
代名詞	主格	所有格	受格
I	I	my	me
She	She	her	her
He	He	his	him
Who	Who	whose	whom

代名詞的格主要是配合它在句子中擺在主詞、受詞或是所有詞的位置來決定，例如：

5. **He was 19 years old in 2010.**

He（主詞）→主格

2010 年時他 19 歲。

6. **John Lin lost his wallet yesterday.**

his（所有詞）→所有格

林約翰昨天遺失了他的皮包。

7. **Mary Lin told him to go home.**

him（受詞）→受格

林瑪麗叫他回家。

在《經濟學人》的文章中介紹一位人物時，第一次是用他／她的全名〔first name（given name）＋last name（family name）〕做介紹，第二次出現時才會用頭銜加上他／她的姓（last name/family name）做後續的報導，此時讀者就不用去猜測到底哪一個字才是姓或名，因為人名第二次出現時就是姓了，例句如下：

Yoshihiko Noda was appointed by the Emperior as Japan's prime minister on September 2nd, 2011. Prime Minister Noda will face challenging tasks of rebuilding Japan after the March earthquake.

日本天皇在 2011 年 9 月 2 日任命野田佳彥為日本首相，野田首相將面臨三月地震之後重建日本的挑戰。

在例句中 Yoshihiko Noda（野田佳彥）為全名，讀者或許不了解到底 Noda 是姓或是 Yoshihiko 是姓，但是不用擔心，在第二句時用 Prime Minister Noda（野田首相）做開頭時，讀者就可知道 Noda 是姓，Yoshihiko 是名了，再看下面的例句：

Paul Krugman of Princeton University had won the Nobel Prize in Economics in 2008. Mr. Krugman is known as the expert in international economics.

普林斯頓大學的保羅‧克魯曼榮獲 2008 年的諾貝爾經濟學獎，克魯曼先生是國際經濟學的專家。

在上述的例句，以全名 Paul Krugman 介紹主角出場，第二句才以 Mr. Krugman 介紹克魯曼的專長領域。這樣讀者就了解 Paul Krugman 的姓是 Krugman，名是 Paul 了。

1-2 練習

▶ 請將下列句中的代名詞找出來。

1. Lula has given an advice to his staff.

2. Boeing and Airbus had demonstred their latest planes at the Paris Air Show.

3. The United States has starting to withdraw its troop from Iraq on October 1st, 2010.

4. Mary Lin, whose house was destroyed by wild fire, was seeking help.

5. Japan's government is expected to keep its budget deficit to around 30% of GDP.

6. On average rich country governments now have much higher debt-to-GDP rations than their emerging countries.

7. Robert Huai has more interesting career in Citibank's Taipei branch. He is the acting director of the bank.

8. Mary catched a monkey at her backyard. It was taken to the local pet shelter.

9. Barack Obama has starting his campaign tour on Monday. President Obama is expected to announce his 2012 campaign plans on the road.

10. The National Rifle Association (NRA) has called its members to boycotte the local election.

1-2 解答

1. *his*

中譯:魯拉提供建議給其職員。

2. *their*

中譯:波音和空中巴士在法國巴黎航空展上展示他們最新的飛機。

3. *its*

中譯:美國從 2010 年 10 月 1 日開始從伊拉克撤軍。

4. *whose*

中譯:房子被野火所毀的林瑪麗在尋求幫助。

5. *its*

中譯:日本政府預期將預算赤字維持在國內生產毛額的 30% 左右。

6. *their*

中譯:一般來說,先進國家政府負債占國內生產毛額的比率都比開發中國家來的高。

7. *He*

中譯:勞勃胡在臺北花旗銀行擁有有趣的職涯發展,他現在是分行的代理經理。

8. *her, It*

中譯:瑪麗在她家後院捉到一隻猴子,她把牠帶到當地的動物收容所。

9. *President Obama, his*

中譯:歐巴馬在星期一展開他的競選之旅,歐巴馬總統預期在競選之旅中宣布他的 2012 年競選連任活動。

10. *its*

中譯:全國步槍協會呼籲其會員杯葛地方選舉。

■1.3 形容詞

形容詞主要用在「形容」名詞，因此要擺在名詞之前「形容」它所要的名詞。例如：

Mary Lin is a good girl.
　　　　　　 adj

林瑪麗是一位好女孩。

在例句中，我們用形容詞 good 來形容名詞 girl，讓整個句子從單調的句型，變成有形容詞裝飾的句型。

要形容一個名詞不限定只能用一個形容詞，也可以連續用好幾個形容詞來形容，但是記得要在最後一個形容詞之前用連接詞 and 來表示連續性形容詞的結束。

例如：

Mary Lin is a beautiful and good girl.
　　　　　　　 adj　　　　 *adj*

林瑪麗是一位美麗又好的女孩。

在例句中，我們用 beautiful 與 good 二個形容詞來形容 girl，但是用連接詞 and 來連接，至於由分詞轉型為形容詞的用法，則留在第四章才做討論。

🖊 1-3 練習

▶ 請將下列句子中的形容詞找出來。

1. Kenya was experiencing a painful political reform.

2. Many Africans, who have been tested for HIV positive, did not know that severe pain can be relieved.

3. The sky of Yemen was covered by dark cloud when the wild fire broke out last month.

4. The Kremlin has either replaced or fired the most powerful local leaders over the past 18 months when Dmitry Medevedev took power in 2008.

5. Peace talks between Palestine and Israel have been halt by difficult issues.

6. Informal talks between President Chavez of Venezuela and opposition leaders have hit a rough patch.

7. Cheap, small and simple cars are designed by many automatic design houses around the world.

8. Declines in interest rates in developed countries have caused currency markets' recent volatility.

9. The prices of precious metals, for example gold and silver, have increased by 50% in recent months. Strong demands from the emerging countries will push the price to the higher level.

10. Apple Inc. will launch an expensive version of iPhone 4.0 at annual International Consumer Electronics Show (CES) at Las Vegas, U.S.A.

📖 1-3 解答

1. *painful, political*

   中譯：肯亞經歷了痛苦的政治改革。

2. *severe*

   中譯：許多有 HIV 陽性反應的非洲民眾不知道這些痛苦可以解除。

3. *dark, wild*

   中譯：上個月野火火災之後，葉門的上空被黑煙所覆蓋。

4. *powerful, local*

   中譯：當迪瑪催・梅帝弟在 2008 年掌權時，克里姆林宮對當地的政治領導人物不是開除，就是找人替代。

5. *difficult*

   中譯：巴勒斯坦和以色列的和談因為許多困難的問題而停頓。

6. *Informal, rough*

   中譯：委內瑞拉總統查維茲和反對黨的非正式談判崎嶇難行。

7. *Cheap, small and simple, automatic*

   中譯：全球許多汽車設計公司設計便宜、小型和簡單的汽車。

8. *recent*

   中譯：已開發國家不斷下降的利率造成最近外匯市場的波動。

9. *precious, recent*

   中譯：黃金和白銀這類貴金屬的價格最近上漲了 50%，開發中國家的強烈需求將會使得價格更加上漲。

10. *expensive, annual*

    中譯：蘋果公司將在美國拉斯維加斯年度消費電子展上推出較貴的 iPhone 4.0 產品。

■1.4 動詞

動詞是英文句型的靈魂，每一個句子中都必須要有動詞的存在，才能形成完整的結構，例如：

Mary Lin is a good girl.

　　　V

林瑪麗是一位好女孩。

在例句中，is 是本句中的動詞。有時在句子中主詞直接省略，用動詞做句首，形成命令句的結構，例如：

Open your book.

　V

打開你的書。

或是

Stand up.

　V

起立。

通常動詞擺在句子的中間，因此只要找到動詞後便可以知道動詞的前面是主詞，動詞的後面便是受詞，例如：

President Barack Obama was heading for Beijing, China, for

　　　　　S.　　　　　　　　V.　　　　　　　　O

G20 summit.

歐巴馬總統啟程前往中國北京參加 20 大工業國高峰會。

在上述例句中，動詞為 was heading for，其前面便是主詞 President Barack Obama，而動詞的後面便是受詞 Beijing, China, for G20 summit。

一個句子中只能有一個動詞，如果要放置二個以上的動詞時，就必須有連接詞來做連接的動作，句子才能成立。例如：

Mary Lin is watch TV. ....(×)

　　S　　　V　　O

林瑪麗看電視。

在上述的例句中，is 是動詞（be 動詞），watch（一般動詞）也是動詞，因此句子的結構是錯誤的，要修正為下列的句型才是正確的。

Mary Lin is watching TV. ....(o)
$\quad\quad$ S $\quad\quad$ V $\quad\quad$ O

林瑪麗正在看電視。

將 watch 改寫為 watching 現在進行式的結構才是正確的。再看下列的例句：

Mary Lin watched TV and washed clothes yesterday.
$\quad$ S $\quad\quad$ V $\quad\quad\quad\quad$ V $\quad\quad\quad\quad$ O

林瑪麗昨天看電視和洗衣服。

在上述例句中有二個動詞，分別是 watched 是動詞，washed 也是動詞，但是有連接詞 and 介於其中，因此在文法上沒有問題。

動詞有 be 動詞和一般動詞二種，同時根據時態和句型結構的不同，又可區分為現在式、過去式和過去分詞的型態，如表 1-2 所示。一般動詞又可區分為規則變化和不規則變化。

表1-2　動詞三態變化

		現在式	過去式	過去分詞
be 動詞	am	am	was	
	is	is	was	
	are	are	were	
一般動詞	規則變化 wash／watch	wash watch	washed watched	washed watched
	不規則變化 see／hear	see hear	saw hard	seen hard

其實要找出英文新聞或雜誌句子中的動詞非常的簡單，因為報章雜誌所報導的事件都是過去式或是即將發生的事件（有助動詞 will 或 shall 的存在），因此只要找到句子中單字字尾加上 ed 的單字，90% 就是該句子中的動詞了，例句如下：

The Bank of Japan (BOJ) announced that it would maintain
         S.   *V.*   *O.*

zero-rate policy.

日本中央銀行宣布零利率政策。

在句子中，只有 announced 是字尾加 ed，因此可以判定 announced 是動詞，The Bank of Japan 是主詞，that it would maintain zero-rate policy 是受詞。

另外，一個找出動詞的方法，便是從不定詞片語來著手，不定詞片語為 to 加上原形動詞（to＋v）成為名詞，作為句子中的主詞或受詞之用。

♦ 1-4 練習

▶ 請將下列句子中的動詞找出來（部分句子有二個以上的動詞）。

1. Japan's economy had rebounced in 2009.

2. Japanese politicians called Prime Minister Yukio Hatoyama to step down.

3. The Bank of Japan (BOJ) was willing to respond a decline economy in hurry.

4. The Nikkei 225 stock index hit a three-month high on September 12nd after the zero-rate policy announcement.

5. The debate over universal values in China has wildly spreaded in the country.

6. The United States and Japan trimed interest rates and flooded the market with cheap money.

7. The battle against online music and video piracy has heating up in recent months.

8. Governments around the world tended to ignore one of their basic responsibilites, education.

9. Michael Jordan announced that he will retire from the sport at the end of 2005 season.

10. Tiger Woods beat his rivals and won the British Open in 2008.

📖 1-4 解答

1. *had rebounced*
   中譯：日本經濟在 2009 年反彈。

2. *called, step down*
   中譯：日本政治人物要求首相鳩山由紀夫下臺。

3. *was, respond*
   中譯：日本中央銀行願意趕快針對衰退的經濟採取行動。

4. *hit*
   中譯：在零利率政策宣布後日經 225 指數在 9 月 12 日上漲到三個
   月的新高。

5. *has, spreaded*
   中譯：有關普世價值的爭論在中國已經展開。

6. *trimed, flooded*
   中譯：美國和日本降低利率的同時，讓大量的貨幣在市場上流動。

7. *has*
   中譯：最近幾個月來，對抗網路音樂和電腦盜版的活動正展開。

8. *tended, ignore*
   中譯：全球的政府都忽略了其基本的責任，那就是教育。

9. *announced, retire*
   中譯：邁可‧喬登宣布在 2005 年球季結束後將退休。

10. *beat, won*
    中譯：老虎伍茲打敗對手贏得 2008 年英國公開賽。

■1.5 副詞

副詞的用途在於形容動詞和形容形容詞，因此副詞要擺在形容詞和動詞的前面，例如：

Mary Lin is a very good girl.
$\qquad\qquad$ *adv.*

林瑪麗是一位非常好的女孩。

在例句中，我們用副詞 very 來形容 good，使得原本句子的林瑪麗是一位「好女孩」變成比較有特色的「非常好的女孩」。

副詞用來形容動詞通常擺在一般動詞的前面，或是擺在 be 動詞的後面，例如：

Mary Lin usually wakes up at 6 o'clock.
$\qquad\quad$ *adv.*

林瑪麗通常在 6 點鐘起床。

Mary Lin was deeply unhappy with government's debt
$\qquad\qquad\quad$ *adv.*
 reduction plan.

林瑪麗非常不滿意政府的債務刪減計畫。

要找出副詞比較簡單，只要單字字尾有 ly，80% 就是副詞了。例如：cleary, slowly, truly, happily 或 fully。有時副詞也會擺在句首修飾全句，例如：

Certainly, Mary Lin is a very good girl.
 adv. $\qquad\qquad\qquad$ *adv.*

當然林瑪麗是一位非常好的女孩，無庸置疑。

在例句中，我們用 Certainly 來修飾全句。

副詞有時擺在句子的最後，表示時間的狀態，例如：

Mitt Romney, a former governor of Massachusetts, is running the Republican presidential primary day and night.
$\qquad\qquad\qquad\qquad\qquad\qquad$ 時間副詞

美國麻州前州長米特‧羅姆尼日以繼夜的參加共和黨的總統黨內初選。

在例句的句尾，我們用時間副詞 day and night 說明主詞 Mitt Romney 參選美國共和黨黨內總統初選的激烈情況。《經濟學人》常見的副詞，如表 1-3 所示。

表1-3　常用副詞

頻率副詞		字尾 ly 副詞		時間副詞	
always	總是	closely	密切的	in the morning	在早上
never	從來不	really	真實的	at night	在晚上
rarely	很少	kindly	好心的	every day	每天
usually	總是	heavily	沉重的	day after day	日復一日
sometimes	有時	slowly	慢慢的	day and night	日以繼夜
often	時常	quickly	快速的	late	來不及
hardly	幾乎不	early	提早	in years	多年來

1-5 練習

▶ 請將下列句子中的副詞找出來。

1. Nicolas Sarkozy, France's president, said that German-style labour reforms couldn't never take place in France.

2. Vladimir Putin, Russia's prime minister, says that Russia's economy can't always depend on oil and natural gas.

3. Irag's Sunni party returned to parliament and would start to talk with Shia leaders.　Sunni and Shia leaders rarely discuss Irag's future in the parliament.

4. The International Atomic Energy Agency (IAEA) closely watches Japan's plan to restart some of the nuclear reactors.

5. America's economy slowly grew by 1.0% in the final quarter of 2011.

6. Starbucks, America's coffeehouse chain, is really taking India's market. It will open its first coffee shop in a joint venture with Tata, a giant conglomerate.

7. The European Commission blocked a merger between NYSE Euronext and Deutsche Börse, mostly over competition concerns.

8. Facebook began the process of launching its initial public offering (IPO) in the most awaited market flotation in years.

9. American Airlines heavily saddles with debt and files for Chapter 11 bankruptcy protection.

10. Twitter often known as the guard of free speech in the cyberworld starts to censor its content in countries where it breaks local laws .

1-5 解答

1. *never*
   中譯：法國總統薩柯琪說德國模式的勞動改革不可能永遠不在法國發生。

2. *always*
   中譯：俄羅斯總理蒲亭說俄羅斯的經濟不能總是依賴石油和天然氣。

3. *rarely*
   中譯：伊拉克的遜尼派回到國會，並且可能和什葉派領導人展開和談。遜尼派和什葉派領導人很少在國會上討論伊拉克的未來。

4. *closely*
   中譯：國際原子能總署密切的觀察日本重新啟動核能反應爐的計畫。

5. *slowly*
   中譯：美國經濟在 2011 年第四季慢慢的成長 1%。

6. *really*
   中譯：美國咖啡連鎖店星巴克真的進軍印度，它將和印度大企業塔塔合資開設第一家分店。

7. *mostly*
   中譯：歐洲委員會禁止紐約證交所歐洲版和德國證交所的合併案，反對的主要理由是產業競爭的因素。

8. *in years*
   中譯：臉書在多年來期待下，終於開始申請股票上市的作業。

9. *heavily*
   中譯：美國航空公司在承受大筆負債壓力下，申請破產保護。

10. *often*
    中譯：在網路世界以捍衛言論自由的推特，開始在某些國家審查其發文的內容，以免違反當地法令。

■1.6 介系詞

介系詞主要在表現句子中所描述場景的時間和地點,介系詞(in, at, on, of⋯)通常擺在句子中的句尾,用來描述主詞和動詞所發生的時間或地點,例如:

Mary Lin was a very good girl in 1990s.

prep

林瑪麗在 1990 年代是一位很好的女孩。

在例句中,我們用介系詞 in 來突顯主詞林瑪麗是在 90 年代的好。

American troops in Iraq are starting to withdraw from the

prep

country on September 1st, 2010.

prep

從 2010 年 9 月 1 日美軍開始撤出伊拉克。

在例句中,我們用二個介系詞 in 和 on 來突顯美軍在伊拉克的軍隊和撤軍的日期在 2010 年 9 月 1 日。

雖然介系詞在英文句子中擺在句尾,但是在中文翻譯時卻必須擺在句首以符合中文的寫作習慣。

介系詞中最常見的就是 of 了,of 常用來代表無生命物品的所有格,其典型句型為 A of B,中文為 B 的 A,例如:

the legs of table 中文翻譯為桌子的腳,因此例句為:

prep

The legs of table are broken by force.

prep

桌腳被外力破壞了。

of 前面要接名詞,後面也要接名詞,在 of 的片語用法中要注意的是主角,of 前面的名詞才是主角,因此在上述的例句中主詞是 The legs,因此動詞要用複數動詞 are。

1-6 練習

▶ 請將下列句子中的介系詞找出來。

1. In the emerging world, the equity markets have reached a three-month high at the end of third quarter.

2. China's trade surplus was coming from export-oriented industries in the late 1990s.

3. President Obama greeted the G20 leaders at the South Lawn of the White House.

4. South Korea's Samsung group announced a 110 billion investment in Iran's gas pipeline project.

5. Citibank will complete its restructure process before the beginning of 2011.

6. After the mid-term election, Democratic party lost its American Congress majority.

7. Kraft group reported a 20% growth in sales revenue in the first half of 2010.

8. The IMF stated that the world economy grew at 2% which was above the forecasted 1% growth at the end of second half of 2010.

9. Microsoft's mobil operating system is not wildly used in the smartphone market.

10. On October 10th, HTC is due to realease a series of smartphone in North American markets.

📖 1-6 解答

1. *in, at*
   中譯：新興國家的股票市場在第三季結束時達到三個月來的新高。

2. *in*
   中譯：在 1990 年代末期，中國的外匯存底主要來自出口導向的產業。

3. *at, of*
   中譯：歐巴馬總統在白宮南草坪接待 20 大工業國的領袖。

4. *in*
   中譯：南韓三星集團宣布在伊朗投資 1,100 億的天然氣運輸管線案。

5. *before, of*
   中譯：花旗銀行在 2011 年初之前將完成其組織改造計畫。

6. *After*
   中譯：在期中選舉之後，民主黨喪失在美國參議院多數黨的地位。

7. *in, in, of*
   中譯：卡夫特集團宣布 2010 年上半年的營業額增加20%。

8. *at, above, at*
   中譯：國際貨幣基金會發表 2010 年下半年世界經濟成長率為 2%，高於當初預估的 1% 成長率。

9. *in*
   中譯：微軟手機作業系統在智慧型手機市場中沒有廣泛的被採用。

10. *On, of, in*
    中譯：宏達電在 10 月 10 日將在北美市場發表一系列的智慧型手機。

■1.7 連接詞

連接詞在英文句子結構中,主要扮演二個相同詞性(動詞、形容詞……)單字的連接工作,或是二個句子的連接工作,例如:

Mary Lin is a good and beautiful girl.

conj

林瑪麗是一位好的和美麗的女孩。

在例句中,我們用連接詞 and 來連接前面的形容詞 good 和後面的形容詞 beautiful。接下來,我們來看下面的例句:

Mary Lin is not only a good girl but also a good student.

conj   conj

林瑪麗不僅是一位好女孩,也是一位好學生。

在例句中,我們用連接詞 not only-but also 來連接前面的受詞 a good girl 和後面的受詞 a good student。

接下來,我們看一下用連接詞 and 連接二個句子的句子,例如:

Mary Lin is a good girl and her little sister is a good girl, too.

conj

林瑪麗是一位好女孩,她妹妹也是一位好女孩。

在例句中,我們用連接詞 and 連接第一句 Mary Lin is a good girl,和連接第二句 her little sister is a good girl, too.

1-7 練習

▶ 請找出下列句子中的連接詞。

1. Steve Jobs directly oversees the iPhone design and development at Apple Inc.

2. The phone is not only a phone but also a platform for thousands of applications.

3. Ford Co. spent $100 million to upgrade its plants, and it saved the company in the long run.

4. Chicago and its surrounding counties have suffered the biggest economic downturn during the 2008 financial crisis.

5. It is either a boy or a girl.

6. Mary neither drinks beer nor eats meat.

7. This year's Nobel Prize in Chemistry has been awarded to chemists Richard Heck, Ei-ichi Negishi and Akira Suzuki.

8. Mexico's full size of the federal police is 40,000 and 4,000 were let go because of corruption.

9. America's President Obama as well as British's Prime Minister Cameron is facing the mid-term election later this month.

10. Both Lady Gaga and Madonna are scheduled to show up at 2010 MTV award ceremony.

1-7 解答

1. *and*

中譯：賈伯斯直接指導蘋果公司 iPhone 的開發和設計。

2. *not only, but also*

中譯：這支手機不只是手機，也是數以千計應用軟體的使用平臺。

3. *and*

中譯：福特汽車公司花費 1 億美元更新其工廠，這樣做有助於該公司長期發展。

4. *and*

中譯：芝加哥和其周遭地區在 2008 年金融危機中遭受最嚴重的經濟衰退。

5. *either, or*

中譯：它不是男性就是女性。

6. *neither, nor*

中譯：瑪麗不喝啤酒也不吃肉。

7. *and*

中譯：今年諾貝爾化學獎頒發給化學家雷查・海克、根岸英一和鈴木章。

8. *and*

中譯：墨西哥警員人數共有 40,000 人，其中有 4,000 人因為貪污被解職。

9. *as well as*

中譯：美國總統歐巴馬和英國首相喀麥隆在月底都必須面對期中選舉。

10. *both, and*

中譯：Lady 卡卡和瑪丹娜都將出席 2010 年 MTV 頒獎典禮。

■1.8 感嘆詞

　　感嘆詞顧名思義用來表示全句的感嘆、驚嘆、惋惜或喜、怒、哀、樂等情緒，感嘆句通常擺在句首達到畫龍點睛之效，例如：

Wow! Mary Lin is a good girl.
　iterj

哇！林瑪麗是一位好女孩。

再看下一句：

Congratulations, you have been prompted.
　　　　interj

恭喜你，升官了。

有時感嘆句只有一個單字的存在，表示驚嘆的成分，例如：

★ Yummy！好吃！

★ Hip, hip, hooray！歡呼

★ Bravo！讚

★ Hey！嗨

★ Ouch！痛

★ Boo！不滿（噓聲）

★ My God！天啊

★ Bye！再見

★ Alas！唉！

★ Hello！幸會

★ Hurrah！好哇

★ Thank you. 謝謝你

🖊 1-8 練習

▶ 請將下列句子中的感嘆詞找出來。

1. Hello, nice to meet you.

2. Bravo, 33 Chile miners have been rescued.

3. Yummy, this is the best Chinese food I ever have.

4. See you next week. Bye!

5. Boo! The France national soccer team failed their people in the World Cup in South Africa.

6. Three cheers for the team: Hip, hip, hooray.

7. Walmart's employee T-shirts read: Thank you.

8. My God! That is a real magic bullet.

9. Ouch! The rising oil price is hurting my wallet.

10. Alas, I must leave now.

1-8 解答

1. *Hello*

   中譯：你好，真高興看到你。

2. *Bravo*

   中譯：讚，受困的 33 名智利礦工已被救出。

3. *Yummy*

   中譯：這是我吃過最好吃的中國菜。

4. *Bye*

   中譯：下星期見，再見。

5. *Boo*

   中譯：噓！法國國家足球隊在南非舉辦的世界杯足球賽中讓法國人失望。

6. *Hip, hip, hooray*

   中譯：大家為這支隊伍歡呼三次。

7. *Thank you*

   中譯：威瑪量販的員工背心上寫著：謝謝你。

8. *My God*

   中譯：天啊，這真是奇蹟。

9. *Ouch*

   中譯：真是痛心，上升的油價讓我荷包縮水。

10. *Alas*

    中譯：唉，我現在就必須走了。

英文單字的詞性當然不止這八種，例如由動詞轉化成分詞或動名詞等，我們會在後續的章節中加以討論。

第一章 綜合練習

▶ 請將下列文章中的單字按照其詞性，填入下列空格中。

There are many tough times ahead for the offspring of corporate legends. Bill Ford of Ford Co. and Umberto Agnelli of Fiat Co. are both struggling to keep alive the huge public companies, which were founded by their founding fathers several decades ago. On September 17th, 2003, Christopher Galvin, who is the grandson of the founder of Motorola, finally gave up his struggle. He submitted his resignation as chairman of the falling mobile phone giant to the company's board. The board announced it publicly two days later. Bravo! Investors cheered. Motorola's share price, which reached the lowest point of its history, rose by 10% after the statement was announced. David Kay who is the senior analyst of Goldman Sachs thinks that the days of Galvin family are numbered. Motorola may be run by professional managers appointed by the board later this month.

名詞	代名詞	形容詞	動詞	副詞	介系詞	連接詞	感嘆詞

第一章 綜合練習解答

名詞	代名詞	形容詞	動詞	副詞	介系詞	連接詞	感嘆詞
times	there	corporate	are	finally	ahead	and	bravo
offspring	which	many	keep	publicly	of	both	
legends	their	alive	gave up	later	on		
Bill Ford	who	huge	submitted		as		
Ford Co.	his	public	announced		by		
Umberto Agnelli	he	several	cheered		after		
Fiat Co.	it	ago	reached		for		
Companies	its	senior	rose				
fathers	that	professional	was				
decades	this		were				
Christopher Galvin			founded				
struggle			announced				
grandson			thinks				
founder			numbered				
Motorola			may				
resignation			be				
chairman			is				
mobile			run				
phone			appointed				
giant							
company's							
board							
days							
investors							
share							
price							
point							
history							
statement							
David Kay							
Analyst							
Goldman Sachs							
days							
Galvin family							
managers							
month							

第一章 單字

- ★economy 經濟
- ★hand over 交棒
- ★Brazil 巴西
- ★President Lula 魯拉總統
- ★dawn of nuclear age 核能時代的來臨
- ★headquarters 企業總部
- ★wealth management 財富管理
- ★asset management 資產管理
- ★expertise 專長
- ★Lehman Brothers 雷曼兄弟
- ★join military exercise 聯合軍事演習
- ★growth engine 成長引擎
- ★emerging nations 新興國家
- ★in the next decade 下一個世代
- ★available 有空的
- ★Boeing 波音
- ★Airbus 空中巴士
- ★troop 軍隊
- ★Iraq 伊拉克
- ★withdraw 撤出
- ★wild fire 野火
- ★budget deficit 預算赤字
- ★GDP 國內生產毛額
- ★rich country governments 富有國家的政府
- ★debt-to-GDP ratios 負債占國內生產毛額的比率
- ★career 職業
- ★Citibank 花旗銀行
- ★pet shelter 寵物收容所
- ★campaign tour 競選活動之旅
- ★announce 宣布
- ★The National Rifle Association (NRA) 國家步槍協會
- ★boycott 杯葛
- ★Kenya 肯亞
- ★political reform 政治改革
- ★Africans 非洲民眾
- ★HIV positive HIV陽性反應
- ★Yemen 葉門
- ★The Kremlin 克里姆林宮（俄羅斯權力中心）
- ★peace talks 和談
- ★Palestine 巴勒斯坦
- ★Israel 以色列
- ★halt 停止
- ★issues 議題
- ★President Chavez of Venezuela 委內瑞拉總統查維茲
- ★decline 下降（衰退）
- ★interest rate 利率
- ★developed countries 已開發國家
- ★cause 造成
- ★currency market 外匯市場
- ★volatility 波動

★precious metal 貴金屬

★emerging countries 新興國家

★Apple Inc. 蘋果公司

★an expensive version 昂貴版

★annual 年度

★International Consumer Electronics Show (CES) 國際消費電子展

★Las Vegas 拉斯維加斯

★President Obama 歐巴馬總統

★G20 20大工業國

★summit 高峰會

★The Bank of Japan (BOJ) 日本中央銀行

★maintain 維持

★zero-rate policy 零利率政策

★rebound 反彈

★politician 政治人物

★Yukio Hatoyama 鳩山由紀夫

★step down 下臺

★hurry 趕快

★The Nikkei 225 stock index 日經 225 股價指數

★debate 爭論

★universal values 普世價值

★spread 散播

★trim 刪減

★flood 散布（流通）

★ignore 忽視

★responsibility 責任

★Tiger Woods 老虎伍茲

★rivals 對手

★the British Open 英國公開賽

★Mitt Romney 米特・羅姆尼

★governor 州長

★the Republican presidential primary 共和黨總統初選

★Nicolas Sarkozy 尼可萊・薩柯琪

★German-style 德國模式

★labour reforms 勞動改革

★Vladimir Putin 浦亭

★Russia 俄羅斯

★prime minister 總理

★oil 原油

★natural gas 天然氣

★Sunni party 遜尼派

★Shia leaders 什葉派領導人

★parliament 國會

★The International Atomic Energy Agency (IAEA) 國際原子能總署

★nuclear reactors 核子反應爐

★final quarter 第四季

★Starbucks 星巴克

★coffeehouse chain 咖啡連鎖店

★India 印度

★a joint venture 合資

★Tata 塔塔 （印度跨國企業）

★conglomerate 多元化的

★The European Commission

歐洲委員會

★block 阻止

★merger 合併

★NYSE Euronext
紐約證交所歐洲版

★Deutsche Borse 德國證交所

★competition 競爭

★concern 考量點

★Facebook 臉書

★launch 展開

★initial public offering (IPO)
股票上市

★await 期待

★flotation 上市

★American Airlines 美國航空公司

★saddle 承擔

★debt 負債

★file 申請

★bankruptcy protection 破產保護

★Twitter 推特

★in the cyberworld 網路世界

★censor 審查

★content 內文

★local laws 當地法律

★equity markets 股票市場

★trade surplus 貿易順差

★export-oriented 出口導向

★the South Lawn of the White
House 白宮南草坪

★South Korea 南韓

★Samsung 三星

★billion 10億

★Iran 伊朗

★gas pipeline 天然氣管線

★restructure 重整

★mid-term election 期中選舉

★American Congress 美國參議院

★majority 多數黨

★Kraft group 卡夫特集團

★sales revenue 營業額

★The IMF 國際貨幣基金會

★forecast 預估

★Microsoft 微軟

★mobile operating system
行動電話作業系統

★smartphone market
智慧型手機市場

★HTC 宏達電

★release 發表

★North American market
北美市場

★Steve Jobs 賈伯斯

★platform 平臺

★applications 應用軟體

★Ford 福特

★upgrade 升級（更新）

★in the long run 長期

★Chicago 芝加哥

★surrounding counties 周圍的郡

★suffer 遭受

★economic downturn 經濟衰退

★financial crisis 金融危機

★Nobel Prize 諾貝爾獎

★award 頒發

★chemist 化學家

★Mexico 墨西哥

★let go 解職

★corruption 貪污

★Prime Minister Cameron
卡麥隆總理

★Lady Gaga Lady 卡卡

★Madonna 瑪丹娜

★award ceremony 頒獎典禮

★Chile 智利

★miners 礦工

★rescue 救援

★the World Cup 世界杯

★soccer 足球

★South Africa 南非

★Walmart 威瑪量販

★employee 員工

★magic bullet 特效藥

★tough time 困難時刻

★offspring 後代

★corporate legends 企業傳奇

★Fiat Co. 飛雅特公司

★public company 股票上市公司

★founding fathers 創辦人

★grandson 孫子

★Motorola 摩托羅拉

★submit 交出

★resignation 辭職

★chairman 董事長

★company's board 公司董事會

★the board 董事會

★share price 股價

★reach 達到

★cheer 歡呼

★investor 投資人

★senior analyst 資深分析師

★Goldman Sachs 高盛

★are numbered 維持不久了

★professional manager
專業經理人

★appoint 指派

第二章 句子結構

在上一章中，我們已經學習了如何用單字的詞性，擺在句子正確的位置上（主詞＋動詞＋受詞）。但是這只是最基本的，畢竟上述的句子結構都是簡單句的結構，對《經濟學人》中的文章而言，大部分的句子結構都是屬於複合句、複雜句、或複合複雜句的型態。一般來說，英文句子的結構可分為四種，分別為簡單句、複合句、複雜句，以及複合複雜句。

■2.1 簡單句

簡單句是英文句子結構中最簡單的句型，其結構分別為主詞＋動詞＋受詞三大部分，其中動詞是一定要有的，而根據新聞英文的寫作型式，大部分的新聞事件，都是已發生的事件，因此動詞都是使用過去式、過去完成式，或是現在完成式，例如：

Egypt managed to attract Foreign Direct Investment (FDI) to
主　　　動　　　　　　　　　　　　　受

the total amount of $50 billion in 2010.

埃及期待在 2010 年吸引了 500 億美元的外國人直接投資。

在上述的句子中，句型結構只有簡單的三個部分，主詞 Egypt、動詞 managed 和受詞 to attract Foreign Direct Investment（FDI）to the total amount of $50 billion in 2010。

再看下列的例句：

A number of 50 projects in infrastructure and public utilities
主

have been offered to private companies by the Egypt government.
動　　　　　　　　　　受

埃及政府提供為數 50 項的公共建設和基礎計畫給私人公司。

在例句中，動詞為現在完成被動的型式 have been offered，而其前面為主詞 A number of 50 projects in infrastructure and public utilities。由於其動詞型態為現在完成被動型式，因此其背後跟著被動句的基本單句由誰 by 來提供這些計畫，主角就是埃及政府 the Egypt government。

再看下列的例句：

The Egypt government's aim in all these infrastructure
主

developments is to secure a promising future for its citizens in
動　　　　　　　　　　受

the desert kingdom.

埃及政府這些基礎建設的動機，就是要給其位在沙漠中王國的國民一個美好的未來。

　　在上述的例句中，動詞是 is，而其前面的主詞是 The Egypt government's aim in all these infrastructure developments 中的 aim，因此動詞用單數的 is，而其後面便是受詞了。

　　在上述的三個例句中，我們可以發現雖然是主詞＋動詞＋受詞的簡單句型，但是每一個單字還是按照我們在第一章中所討論過的八大詞性做分類，有順序而且正確的擺在應該的位置上。

2-1 練習

▶ 找出下列簡單句中的主詞、動詞和受詞。

1. The Egypt government has its eyes on bio-technology industry.
2. London Business School (LBS) offers a wide range of world-class Masters and Executive Education Programs.
3. The International Monetary Fund (IMF) forecasted the world's economy growth rate at 2% in 2009.
4. The World Bank provided $20 billion emergency fund for Nigeria after the 2009 flood.
5. Ten years ago western countries dominated the world economy.
6. Currency wars are going on between developed countries and developing countries.
7. China is unwilling to allow its yuan to appreciate against dollar.
8. Consumer goods are long proven to be recession-proof.
9. China has bad reputation for violations of intellectual property rights.
10. Policymakers around the world determine to smooth the world trade.

2-1 解答

1. 主詞 *The Egypt government*
   動詞 *has*
   受詞 *its eyes on bio-technology industry*
   中譯：埃及政府將其眼光放在生物科技產業上。
2. 主詞 *London Business School (LBS)*
   動詞 *offers*
   受詞 *a wide range of world-class Masters and Executive Education Programs*
   中譯：倫敦商學院提供多面向頂尖的碩士學程和高階主管進修學程。
3. 主詞 *The International Monetary Fund*
   動詞 *forecasted*
   受詞 *the world's economy growth rate at 2% in 2009*
   中譯：國際貨幣基金會預估 2009 年世界經濟成長率為 2%。

4. 主詞 *The World Bank*
   動詞 *provided*
   受詞 *$20 billion emergency fund for Nigeria after the 2009 flood*
   中譯：世界銀行提供 200 億美元緊急基金給經歷 2009 年水患的奈及
   　　　利亞。

5. 主詞 *Ten years ago western countries*
   動詞 *dominated*
   受詞 *the world economy*
   中譯：10 年前西方國家主宰世界經濟。

6. 主詞 *Currency wars*
   動詞 *are going on*
   受詞 *between developed countries and developing countries*
   中譯：貨幣戰爭正在已開發國家和開發中國家間開打。

7. 主詞 *China*
   動詞 *is*
   受詞 *unwilling to allow its yuan to appreciate against dollar*
   中譯：中國不願意讓人民幣對美元升值。

8. 主詞 *Consumer goods*
   動詞 *are long proven*
   受詞 *to be recession-proof*
   中譯：消費性商品長久以來被視為是不受不景氣影響的產業。

9. 主詞 *China*
   動詞 *has*
   受詞 *bad reputation for violations of intellectual property rights*
   中譯：中國違反智慧財產權惡名昭彰。

10. 主詞 *Policymakers around the world*
    動詞 *determine*
    受詞 *to smooth the world trade*
    中譯：全球決策官員決心要使全球貿易更加順暢化。

■2.2 複合句

複合句是由二個句子中間加上連接詞、或分號來組成，其句型結構如下：

主詞1＋動詞1＋受詞1＋連接詞（and, but,……）＋主詞2＋動詞2＋受詞2

複合句的存在主要在補充簡單句於事件說明的不足，運用第二個句子來做補充說明，同時豐富句型的變化，例如：

Egypt managed to attract Foreign Direct Investment (FDI) to
主1　　　動1　　　　　　　　　　　　　　　受1

the total amount of $50 billion in 2010, but the government had
　　　　　　　　　　　　　　　　　　　　連　　　主2　　　　動2

set the target of $60 billion.
　　　　　　受2

埃及在 2010 年期望吸引 500 億美元的外國人直接投資，但是埃及政府的目標是 600 億美元。

在例句中，第一個簡單句和第二個簡單句用對等連接詞 but 來加以連接，而且二個簡單句中分別都有主詞、動詞和受詞。如果把對等連接詞 but 去掉的話，二個句子可以單獨存在，只不過又成為簡單句的結構，例如：

Egypt managed to attract Foreign Direct Investment (FDI) to the total amount of $50 billion in 2010. The government had set the target of $60 billion.

在複合句的閱讀或寫作上要注意二個子句的動詞時態要一致，否則會形成句子前後意思怪怪的感覺，例如：

Mary Lin is a good girl and she was a good student, too. ....(×)
　　　　動1　　　　　　　　　　　動2

林瑪麗現在是好女孩，以前也是一位好學生。

中文的意思完全正確，但是因為對等連接詞 and 的存在，產生英文前後句子時態不一致的錯誤句型，如果改為下列句型就正確了，例如：

Mary Lin was a good girl and she was a good student, too.
　　　　動1　　　　　　　　　　　動2

2-2 練習

▶ 找出下列複合句中的主詞、動詞、受詞和連接詞。

1. The Egypt government has its eyes on bio-technology industry, and it has developed a 300-acre special economic zone for it.

2. London Business School (LBS) offers a wide range of world-class Masters and Executive Education Programs and the programs are taught by the school's faculty.

3. The International Monetary Fund (IMF) forecasted the world's economy growth rate at 2.0% in 2009, but many institutions predicated a 3.0% growth rate.

4. The World Bank provided $20 billion emergency fund for Nigeria after the 2009 flood, and international non-profit organizations offered humanitarian aid.

5. Ten years ago western countries dominated the world economy; the emerging countries may boost the growth after the 2008 credit crunch.

6. Currency wars are going on between developed countries and developing countries, and the currency issue will be the key issue in G20 summit on December, 2010.

7. China is unwilling to allow its yuan to appreciate against dollar, but the U.S. Congress has imposed tariff on China-exported goods.

8. Consumer goods are long proven to be recession-proof, but now consumers prefer store brand goods to name brand goods.

9. China has bad reputation for violations of intellectual property rights, but it files more patent applications than any countries do.

10. Policymakers around the world determine to smooth the world trade, and their leaders are scheduled to meet at the annual conference of the World Trade Organization (WTO).

2-2 解答

1. 主詞 *The Egypt government, it*
   動詞 *has, has developed*
   受詞 *its eyes on bio-technology industry, a 300-acre special economic zone for it*
   連接詞 *and*
   中譯：埃及政府將其眼光放在生物科技產業上，並且為其設立了300公頃的經濟特區。

2. 主詞 *London Business School (LBS), the programs*
   動詞 *offers, are taught*
   受詞 *a wide range of world-class Masters and Executive Education Programs, by the school's faculty*
   連接詞 *and*
   中譯：倫敦商學院提供頂尖的碩士學程和高階主管進修學程，所有課程由學校教授授課。

3. 主詞 *The International Monetary Fund (IMF), many institutions*
   動詞 *forecasted, predicated*
   受詞 *the world's economy growth rate at 2.0% in 2009, a 3.0% growth rate*
   連接詞 *but*
   中譯：國際貨幣基金會預估 2009 年世界經濟成長率為 2%，但是許多機構則預估 3% 的成長率。

4. 主詞 *The World Bank, international non-profit organizations*
   動詞 *provided, offered*
   受詞 *$20 billion emergency fund for Nigeria after the 2009 flood, humanitarian aid*
   連接詞 *and*
   中譯：世界銀行提供 200 億美元的緊急基金給經歷 2009 年水患的奈及利亞，而許多國際非營利組織則提供人道救援協助。

5. 主詞 *western countries, the emerging countries*

動詞 *dominated, may boost*

受詞 *the world economy, the growth after the 2008 credit crunch*

連接詞；

中譯：10 年前西方國家主宰世界經濟，但在 2008 年信用緊縮後新
興國家可能帶動世界經濟成長。

6. 主詞 *Currency wars, the currency issue*

動詞 *are going on, will be*

受詞 *between developed countries and developing countries, the
key issue in G20 summit on December, 2010*

中譯：貨幣戰爭正在已開發國家和開發中國家開打，2010 年 12 月
的 20 大工業國高峰會中，貨幣問題將成為主要的議題。

7. 主詞 *China, the U.S. Congress*

動詞 *is, has imposed*

受詞 *unwilling to allow its yuan to appreciate against dollar, tariff
on China-exported goods*

連接詞 *but*

中譯：中國不願意讓人民幣對美元升值，但是美國國會已對自中國進
口的商品課徵關稅。

8. 主詞 *Consumer goods, consumers*

動詞 *are long proven, prefer*

受詞 *to be recession-proof, store brand goods to name brand
goods*

連接詞 *but*

中譯：消費性商品長久以來被視為是不受不景氣影響的產業，但是現
在消費者偏好量販店自有品牌商品大於著名品牌商品。

9. 主詞 *China, it*

動詞 *has, files*

受詞 *bad reputation for violations of intellectual property rights,
more patent applications than any countries do*

連接詞 *but*

中譯：中國違反智慧財產權惡名昭彰，但是中國比其他國家申請更多
的專利權。

10. 主詞 *Policymakers around the world, their leaders*

動詞 *determine, are scheduled*

受詞 *to smooth the world trade, to meet at the annual conference
of the World Trade Organization (WTO)*

連接詞 *and*

中譯：全球決策官員決心要使全球貿易更加順暢化，他們的領導人
已安排要參加世界貿易組織的年會。

■2.3 複雜句

複雜句主要是二個句子所組成，一般來說，第一個句子叫做主要子句，第二個句子叫做從屬子句。稱為子句因為這二個句子中都要有主詞＋動詞＋受詞的結構，重點是主要子句可以單獨存在成為一個單獨的句子，但是從屬子句卻無法單獨存在，它必須依附在主要子句下才能生存，例如：

China has banned the export of rare earths which are widely
<u>　　　　　　　主要子句　　　　　　　　　　　從屬子句</u>
used in semiconductor industry.

中國禁止在半導體產業廣泛使用之稀土出口。

在上述的例句中，主要子句為中國禁止稀土出口 China has banned the export of rare earths，而從屬子句為稀土廣泛在半導體產業使用 which are widely used in semiconductor industry。

這二個子句中，都分別有主詞 China, which、動詞 has banned, are widely used 和受詞 the export of rare earths, in semiconductor industry。如果我們把主要子句和從屬子句分開的話，就可看出其中文法的錯誤如下：

主要子句：**China has banned the export of rare earths……(o)**

從屬子句：**which is widely used in semiconductor industry……(×)**

在上述的例句中，從屬子句在文法上產生錯誤，因為 which 如果是完整的句子的話，句尾應該是問號（？），如果 which 是肯定句的話，我們也不曉得 which 到底代表誰，形成語意上的混淆。

一般來說，從屬子句可分為三大類，分別是形容詞子句、副詞子句和名詞子句，這三種子句各有其用途和用法，我們在本章中先用形容詞子句來做複雜句的說明，稍後在第三章再針對這三種子句做說明。

在前面的章節中，我們討論過形容詞擺在名詞前面用來形容後面的名詞，例如 a good girl 中的形容詞 good，用來形容後面的名詞 girl。形容詞子句顧名思義就是用一個句子來當作形容詞，形容其前面的名詞，其句型結構如下列二種句型：

(1)主要子句

　　主詞1，關係代名詞（主詞2）＋動詞2＋受詞2，＋動詞1＋受詞1
　　　　　　　　從屬子句（形容詞子句）

Pfizer, which is an American pharmaceutical giant, recalls
　主1　　主2　動2　　　　　　　　受2　　　　　　　　動1

Reductil from the shelf.
　　　　受1

美國大藥廠輝瑞從市場上回收諾美婷。

在例句中，主要子句如下：

Pfizer recalls Reductil from the shelf.
　主1　　動1　　　　受1

而其從屬子句為：

which is an American pharmaceutical giant
　主2　動2　　　　　受2

　　在從屬子句的形容詞子句中的主詞為 which，它是關係代名詞，代表其前面的名詞（主詞）輝瑞 Pfizer、動詞 is 和受詞 an American pharmaceutical giant，這個從屬子句（形容詞子句）主要用來向讀者說明主詞輝瑞 Pfizer 公司的背景資料，讓讀者從閱讀中馬上就知道輝瑞 Pfizer 是一家美國籍的製藥大廠，不必再去閱讀下一句或是查資料才知道輝瑞在從事什麼行業，當然我們也可將上述複雜句改寫成二個簡單句，如下：

Pfizer recalls Reductil from the shelf.
It is an American pharmaceutical giant.

　　但是這二種簡單句的說明和意思與複雜句的說明完全一樣，卻違反了英文寫作的基本原則：一件事用一個句子可以作說明的話，不要寫二個句子來說明。

　　一般來說，中譯時要先把形容詞子句翻譯，再翻譯主要子句的主詞，這樣才能讓讀者了解真義。如果只是按照句子的順序來翻譯的話，讀者搞不清楚中文意思，同時貽笑大方，一般電腦翻譯軟體都犯了這種錯誤，例句如下：

Pfizer, which is an American pharmaceutical giant, recalls Reductil them from the shelf.

輝瑞它是美國大藥廠從市場上回收諾美婷。……（×）

主要子句和從屬子句（形容詞子句）的另一種句型結構如下所示：

(2)主詞1＋動詞1＋受詞1，關係代名詞（主詞2）＋動詞2＋受詞2
　　　主要子句　　　　　　　　從屬子句（形容詞子句）

Next month, South Korea is hosting the summit of G20, which
　　　　　　　　主1　　　　　動1　　　　　受1　　　　　主2

includes the U.S., Germany, Japan,……and China.
　動2　　　　　　　　　　　　受2

　　下個月南韓將主辦包括美國、德國、日本……和中國參加的 20 大工業國高峰會。

　　在例句中，主要子句如下：

Next month, South Korea is hosting the summit of G20.
　　　　　　　　主1　　　　　動1　　　　　受1

而從屬子句為：

which includes the U.S., Germany, Japan,……and China
　主2　　動2　　　　　　　　　　受2

　　在從屬子句（形容詞子句）的主詞為 which，它是關係代名詞，代表其前面的名詞（受詞）20 大工業國 G20、動詞 includes 和受詞 the U.S., Germany, Japan,……and China。

　　在《經濟學人》的文章中，一般都是用複雜句結構中的形容詞子句來形容主要子句中的主詞，而且無論主詞是人、公司或是事件，都必須運用這種寫作方式來說明，幫助讀者迅速的對新聞故事中的主角了解其背景資料。

2-3 練習

▶ 請將下列句子中的從屬子句（形容詞子句）找出來。

1. China, which holds the world's largest foreign reserve, is misleading the public the nature of currency wars.

2. A record number of teachers, bus drivers and postmen took to the streets of Paris in protest the expected pension reform, which raises the minimum retirement age to 62 from 60.

3. Italy's Northern League, which hosts the world famous design houses, was feeling the downturn of global economy.

4. All European countries, which have average 150% debt-to-GDP ratios, prefer an unhappy status quo to change in pension reform.

5. Walmart, which is a wholesale store and has more than 5,000 "big box" around the world, agreed to provide health care plan for its employees.

6. Proferssor Jouhua Lo of Northwestern University, which is famous for its MBA program, publishes his research paper on the *Journal of Finance*.

7. A bill which was passed by the House of Representatives last month would treat the undervalued currencies as an export subsidy, which was supported by governments.

8. Groupon, which is a social commerce network site, is expected to reach sales revenue of $1 billion in 2010.

9. Steve Hilton, who is British Prime Minister David Cameron's closest advisor, asks the government to cut public spending by 20%.

10. Ford Foundation, which is a think tank and is based in Washington, D.C., issued American foreign policy review.

2-3 解答

1. *which holds the world's largest foreign reserve*
   中譯：持有全球最多外匯存底的中國，誤導大眾有關貨幣戰爭的本質。

2. *which raises the minimum retirement age to 62 from 60*
   中譯：破紀錄的教師、公車駕駛和郵差在巴黎街頭示威，抗議要將最低退休年齡從 60 歲調高到 62 歲的退休改革計畫。

3. *which hosts the world famous design houses*
   中譯：擁有全球多家著名設計公司的義大利北方聯盟，也感受到全球的經濟衰退。

4. *which have average 150% debt-to-GDP ratios*
   中譯：平均公債占國內生產毛額達 150% 的歐洲各國，對於退休改革喜歡維持現狀大於改變。

5. *which is a wholesale store and has more than 5,000 "big box" around the world*
   中譯：全球擁有超過 5,000 家分店的威瑪量販，同意提供員工健保計畫。

6. *which is famous for its MBA program*
   中譯：以企管碩士教育著名的西北大學教授約華．羅，在《金融學報》上發表其研究著作。

7. *which was passed by the House of Representatives last month, which was supported by governments.*
   中譯：上個月美國眾議院通過法案，將低估的貨幣視為由政府支持的出口補貼。

8. *which is a social commerce network site*
   中譯：團購社群網站「團購」，預估 2010 年營業額將高達 10 億美元。

9. *who is British Prime Minister David Cameron's closest advisor*
   中譯：和英國首相關係密切的顧問史帝芬．希爾頓，要求政府刪減公共支出 20%。

10. *which is a think tank and is based in Washington, D.C.*
    中譯：位在美國華府的智庫福特基金會發表美國外交政策評論。

■2.4 複合複雜句

複合複雜句顧名思義就是將複合句和複雜句結合起來，形成比較複雜的句型結構，但是重點為不論是二個主要子句或是從屬子句，都必須遵守基本的句型結構，也就是要有主詞＋動詞＋受詞的結構，複合複雜句的典型結構如下：

主要子句1

主詞，關係代名詞（主詞）＋動詞＋受詞，＋動詞＋受詞＋連接詞

從屬子句

＋主詞＋動詞＋受詞

主要子句2

在本節中，我們先以形容詞子句（從屬子句）來做說明，例句如下：

The German Federal Ministry of Economics and Technology,

主1

which is responsible for setting industry policy, has recognized

主3　動3　　　　　　　　　　　　受3　　　　　　　　　　　　　動1

the electric car potential and it has established a strategic

受1　　　　　　　　　　　主2　　動2　　　　　受2

alliance with BMW, VW and Mercedes-Benz.

負責制定產業政策的德國聯邦經建部體認到電動車的潛力，已經和寶馬、福斯和賓士建立策略聯盟。

在例句中，我們可找出二個主要子句分別是：

The German Federal Ministry of Economics and Technology has recognized the electric car potential 和 it has established a strategic alliance with BMW, VW and Mercedes-Benz。

中間用連接詞 and 來連接二個主要子句，而從屬子句（形容詞子句）which is responsible for setting industry policy 則是用來形容其前面的主詞 The German Federal Ministry of Economics and Technology 的角色。

我們可以將其改寫成簡單句的句型，便可了解其中的意義，如下：

1. **The German Federal Ministry of Economics and Technology has recognized the electric car potential.**
   德國聯邦經建部體認到電動車的潛力。

2. **It is responsible for setting industry policy.**
   它（聯邦經建部）負責制定產業政策。

3. **It has established a strategic alliance with BMW, VW and Mercedes-Benz.**
   它已和寶馬、福斯和賓士建立策略聯盟。

我們再看下面的例句：

America's relationship with Pakistan is based on carrot and
<u>　　　　主1　　　　</u>　　　　<u>動1</u>　　<u>受1</u>

stick, but President Obama has frequently used carrots, which
<u>　　　　主2　　　</u>　　　　<u>動2</u>　　　<u>受2</u>　<u>主3</u>

include military and monetary aid.
<u>動3</u>　　　　<u>受3</u>

　　美國和巴基斯坦的關係是建立在胡蘿蔔和棒子的方法上，但是歐巴馬總統則經常使用包括軍事和金錢援助的胡蘿蔔方法。

　　在例句中，我們先寫出二個主要子句，分別是：
America's relationship with Pakistan is based on carrot and stick 和 President Obama has frequently used carrots 中間用連接詞 but 來連接，而用從屬子句（形容詞子句） which include military and monetary aid 來形容前面的受詞 carrots（胡蘿蔔），同時說明胡蘿蔔的內容是什麼，也就是軍事和金錢上的援助。

2-4 練習

▶ 請將下列複合複雜句的主詞、關係代名詞和二個主要子句的動詞找出來。

1. Next month, President Obama is heading to India, where he will meet India Prime Minister Manmohan Singh, and then President Obama will fly to Indnesia to meet his early childhood friends.

2. After world War II (WW II), John Maynard Keynes, who was the father of modern economics, provided the growth advice to stimulate the economy, and many governments fellow his advice.

3. Many British cultural institutions aggressively headhunted Americans, who had more experience in fund raising, and the results were significant.

4. Greece, which was bailouted by EU and IMF, has asked China to buy its government bonds, and China has become Greece's largest creditor after purchasing $20 billion bonds.

5. Liu Xiaobo, who is a China's political dissident and is serving eleven years in prison, won the Nobel Peace Prize, but China had blocked the news.

6. Global approval rating of American leadership had been increased, but it has fallen recently according to Gallup, which is a poll firm.

7. President Demitry Medvedev sacked Moscow Mayor Yury Luzhkow and he created a new pro-Medvedev coalition government, which was led by ex-president Vladimir Putin.

8. European life expectancy which is standing 70 years for males and 75 years for females has increased for the last decade, and a later retirement age is unavoidable.

9. Henri Durant, who witnessed the battle of Solferina, helped the wounded soldiers and civilians, and he set up the International committee of the Red Cross, which has more than 97 million volunteers, members and staff worldwide.

10. Zipcar, which was founded by Robin Chase and Antje Danielson in

2000, is an American car-sharing firm, and it has 400,000 members who pay the rent by the hour or day.

📖 2-4 解答

1. 主詞 *President Obama, President Obama*
   關係代名詞 *where*
   動詞 *is heading, will fly*
   中譯：下個月歐巴馬總統將前往印度和印度總理穆哈默・辛赫面談，之後歐巴馬總統將前往印尼拜訪其童年的朋友。

2. 主詞 *John Maynard Keynes, many governments*
   關係代名詞 *who*
   動詞 *provided, fellow*
   中譯：現代經濟學之父凱因斯在第二次世界大戰後提供成長建議，刺激經濟發展，許多政府採用其建議。

3. 主詞 *Many British cultural institutions, the results*
   關係代名詞 *who*
   動詞 *headhunted, were*
   中譯：許多英國文化機構積極聘請有募款經驗的美國人，而且成果輝煌。

4. 主詞 *Greece, China*
   關係代名詞 *which*
   動詞 *has asked, has become*
   中譯：接受歐盟和國際貨幣基金會救援的希臘，要求中國購買其政府公債，中國在購買其 200 億美元公債後，成為希臘最大的債權人。

5. 主詞 *Liu Xiaobo, China*
   關係代名詞 *who*
   動詞 *won, had blocked*
   中譯：正在服 11 年徒刑的中國政治異議者劉曉波獲得諾貝爾和平獎，但是中國卻封鎖該消息。

6. 主詞 *Global approval rating of American leadership, it*

   關係代名詞 *which*

   動詞 *had been increased, has fallen*

   中譯：根據民意調查機構蓋洛普的調查，美國領導力滿意度在過去有
   　　　上升，但是最近又下滑。

7. 主詞 *President Demitry Medvedev, he*

   關係代名詞 *which*

   動詞 *sacked, created*

   中譯：梅帝弟總統撤換莫斯科市長魯內後，成立一個由前總統浦亭所
   　　　領導的親梅帝弟政權。

8. 主詞 *European life expectancy, a later retirement age*

   關係代名詞 *which*

   動詞 *has increased, is*

   中譯：在過去 10 年中歐洲的平均壽命年齡逐漸增加，男性和女性壽
   　　　命分別為 70 歲和 76 歲，延長退休年齡無可避免。

9. 主詞 *Henri Durant, he*

   關係代名詞 *who, which*

   動詞 *helped, set up*

   中譯：杜魯目賭沙飛那戰役後，幫助受傷的軍人和平民百姓，他並且
   　　　設立紅十字會，紅十字會目前在全球有超過 9,700 萬名的志
   　　　工、會員和職員。

10. 主詞 *Zipcar, it*

    關係代名詞 *which, who*

    動詞 *is, has*

    中譯：在 2000 年時羅賓‧查斯和安提‧丹
    　　　尼森創立一家汽車分時共享企業瑞
    　　　車，瑞車目前有會員 400,000 人，會
    　　　員以計時或計日方式支付汽車租金。

第二章 綜合練習

▶ 請將下列文章中的複合句、複雜句、複合複雜句，全部改寫成簡單句。

Qatar Airways, which is the flag carrier of Qatar and is headquartered in the Qatar Airways Tower in Doha, designs premium terminal lounge for first and business class passengers. The lounge is equipped with office facilities and wirelesss connectivity which help premium passengers to keep in touch with ongoing business around the world. On-site staff and attendants provide timely service to meet premium passengers' need and they can enjoy non-stop flying over 90 international destinations. Qatar Airways' excellence has received a 5-star award by Skytrax, which is an airline consulting firm. Despite ongoing tough competition and increasing fuel cost, the airline is one of the fastest growing airlines in the world and it operates the youngest fleets in the industry.

_____

_____

_____

_____

_____

_____

_____

_____

_____

_____

_____

_____

| 第二章 綜合練習解答 |

Qatar Airways designs premium terminal lounge for first and business class passengers. It is the flag carrier of Qatar. It is headquartered in the Qatar Airways Tower in Doha. The lounge is equipped with office facilities and wirelesss connectivity. They help premium passengers to keep in touch with ongoing business around the world. On-site staff and attendants provide timely service to meet premium passengers' need. They can enjoy non-stop flying over 90 international destinations. Qatar Airways' excellence has received a 5-star award by Skytrax. It is an airline consulting firm. Despite ongoing tough competition and increasing fuel cost, the airline is one of the fastest growing airlines in the world. It operates the youngest fleets in the industry.

第二章 單 字

★Egypt 埃及

★Foreign Direct Investment (FDI)
外國人直接投資

★billon 10億

★a number of 為數多少的

★infrastructure 基礎建設

★public utilities 公共建設

★private 私人的

★government 政府

★aim 目標、用心、動機

★development 發展、建設

★secure 確保

★promising 承諾的、美好的

★future 未來

★citizens 國民

★kingdom 王國

★bio-technology 生物科技

★industry 產業

★London Business School (LBS)
倫敦商學院

★offer 提供

★a wild range 多面向的

★world-class 頂尖的世界級

★Masters 碩士

★Executive Education Program
高階主管進修 學程

★The International Monetary
Fund (IMF) 國際貨幣基金會

★forecast 預估

★economy growth rate
經濟成長率

★The World Bank 世界銀行

★provide 提供

★emergency 緊急

★funds 基金、金錢

★Nigeria 奈及利亞

★flood 水災

★western countries 西方國家

★dominate 主宰

★currency wars 貨幣戰爭

★developed countries
已開發國家

★developing countries
開發中國家

★yuan (RMB) 人民幣

★appreciate 升值

★against 對付

★dollar 美元（通稱）

★consumer goods 消費品

★prove 證明

★recession-proof
不受不景氣影響（抗不景氣）

★reputation 名聲、商譽

★violation 違反

★intellectual property rights
智慧財產權

★policymakers 政府決策官員

★determine 下定決心

★acre 公頃

★special economic zone
經濟特區

★faculty 教師

★institutions 機構

★predicate 預估

★international 國際性的

★non-profit organization
非營利組織

★humanitarian aid
人道救援協助

★emerging countries 新興國家

★boost 帶動

★credit crunch 信用緊縮

★key issue 主要議題

★G20 summit
20 大工業國高峰會

★the U.S. Congress 美國國會

★impose 加上

★tariff 關稅

★China-exported goods
自中國進口商品

★prefer 喜歡

★store brand goods
量販店自有品牌商品

★name brand goods
著名品牌商品

★file 申請

★patent applications 專利申請

★schedule 安排

★annual conference 年會

★the World Trade Organization
(WTO) 世界貿易組織

★ban 禁止

★rare earths 稀土

★semiconductor 半導體

★Pfizer 輝瑞

★pharmaceutical giant
製藥大廠

★recalls 回收

★Reductil 諾美婷

★shelf 櫃架、市場

★host 主辦

★foreign reserve 外匯存底

★mislead 誤導

★the public 大眾

★nature 本質

★a record number of 破紀錄的

★protest 示威抗議

★pension reform 退休改革

★retirement 退休

★Italy's Northern League
義大利北方聯盟

★design house 設計公司

★downturn 衰退

★global economy 全球經濟

★European countries 歐洲國家

★debt-to-GDP ratio
公債占國內生產毛額比率

★status quo 現況

★Walmart 威瑪量販
★wholesale store 量販店
★big box 大型量販店
★health-care plan 健保計畫
★employee 員工
★Economics 經濟學
★professor 教授
★Northwestern University 西北大學
★famous for 著名
★MBA 企管碩士
★publish 發表
★research paper 研究著作
★*Journal of Finance* 金融學報
★the House of Representatives 眾議院
★undervalued 低估
★export subsidy 出口補貼
★social commerce network site 團購社群網站
★sales revenue 營業額
★prime minister 首相
★public spending 公共支出
★a think tank 智庫
★Washington, D.C. 美國華府
★foundation 基金會
★foreign policy 外交政策
★review 評論
★recognize 體認、承認
★potential 潛力

★electric car 電動車
★a strategic alliance 策略聯盟
★BMW 寶馬
★VW 福斯
★Mercedes-Benz 賓士
★relationship 關係
★Pakistan 巴基斯坦
★carrot and stick 胡蘿蔔和棒子（獎勵和處罰）
★frequently 經常
★military 軍事
★monetary 金錢（貨幣）
★Prime Minister Manmohan Singh 總理穆哈默·辛赫
★Indonesia 印尼
★childhood 童年
★World War II（WW II）第二次世界大戰
★John Maynard Keynes 凱因斯
★stimulate 刺激
★aggressively 積極
★headhunted 聘請
★fund raising 募款
★results 成果
★significant 輝煌、重大
★Greece 希臘
★bailout 拯救、救援
★EU 歐盟
★government bonds 政府公債
★debtor 債權人

★Liu Xiaobo 劉曉波

★dissident 異議者

★prison 監獄

★the Nobel Peace Prize
　諾貝爾和平獎

★block 封鎖

★approval rating 滿意度

★leadership 領導力

★poll 民意調查

★President Demitry Medvedev
　梅帝弟總統

★sack 撤換

★Moscow 莫斯科

★mayor 市長

★Pro-Medvedev coalition government
　親梅帝弟聯合政權

★ex-president Vladimir Putin
　前總統浦亭

★life expectancy 生命歲數

★male 男性

★female 女性

★unavoidable 無法避免的

★witness 目睹

★battle 戰役

★wounded solider 受傷的軍人

★civilian 平民百姓

★Red Cross 紅十字會

★volunteers 志工

★members 會員

★staff 職員

★car-sharing firm
　汽車分時共享企業

★the rent 租金

★Qatar Airways 卡達航空公司

★the flag carrier 國家航空公司

★Qatar 卡達

★headquartered 總部

★Doha 杜哈（卡達首都）

★premium 頂級的

★terminal lounge
　機場貴賓休息室

★passenger 旅客

★wireless 無線的

★staff 員工

★attendants 服務生

★rare earths 稀土

★non-stop flying 直飛

★destination 目的地

★a consulting firm 顧問公司

★despite 儘管

★competition 競爭

★fleet 機隊（船隊）

第三章 子句

在第二章中，我們討論了英文句子結構可分為簡單句、複合句、複雜句和複合複雜句。在《經濟學人》的句子中，大部分還是屬於複雜句和複合複雜句的結構，這二種句型中除了主要子句外還包括了從屬子句，而從屬子句主要由以下三種所構成，分別是形容詞子句、名詞子句和副詞子句。

形容詞子句、名詞子句和副詞子句這三種子句是英文雜誌寫作的重點，而這三種子句在句子中各有其不同的用途，但是如何分辨從屬子句是形容詞子句、名詞子句或是副詞子句，卻是大多數人的難題，我們來看例句如下：

（1）I know the girl.

　　我認識那位女孩。

（2）I know the girl who is a movie star.

　　　　　　　　　　　形容詞子句

　　我認識的是電影明星的那位女孩。

（3）I know that the girl is a movie star.

　　　　　　名詞子句

　　我知道那位女孩是一位電影明星的事實。

（4）I know the girl because she is a movie star.

　　　　　　　　　　　副詞子句

　　我認識那位女孩，因為她是一位電影明星。

在例句（1）中，是簡單句的結構，有主詞、動詞和受詞，而例句（2）中，卻出現形容詞子句 who is a movie star。在例句（3）有名詞子句 that the girl is a movie star，例句（4）出現了副詞子句 because she is a movie star。相同的主要子句結構 I know the girl，卻加入不同的從屬子句（形容詞子句、名詞子句和副詞子句）來改變句子的說明方式，這三種子句如何區分？大概就是造成大多數英文學習者在閱讀英文新聞時，最受困擾的地方了，如何解開這個難題，請詳閱本章內容。

■3.1 形容詞子句

形容詞子句顧名思義是一個句子,有主詞、動詞和受詞,但是卻用整個句子來形容其前面的名詞,所以才稱之為形容詞子句。比較重要的是,在形容詞子句中的主詞是用關係代名詞來代替前面的名詞,關係代名詞的適用時機如表3-1所示。

表3-1　關係代名詞適用時機

前面的名詞	關係代名詞
主格人稱	who
受格人稱	whom
所有格人稱	whose
物品	which
時間	when
人＋物	that

而形容詞子句中的動詞(單複數)也需配合其主詞的單複數來決定,例句如下:

The Tea Party Movement, which was founded by Trevor
　　　　　　　　　　　　　　主　　　　　　　動
Leach in 2009, is organized to protest against the U.S. federal government's bailout plans for the financial industry.

在 2009 年由泰維‧利區發起成立的茶黨運動,主要是反對美國聯邦政府一連串的金融業紓困計畫。

在句子中,我們用形容詞子句 which was founded by Trevor Leach in 2009,來形容前面的主詞 The Tea Party Movement 茶黨運動的成立背景,由於主要子句中的主詞為物 The Tea Party Movement,所以形容詞子句關係代名詞選用 which,因此動詞用被動的 was founded,再看下面的例句:

The bus driver whom Mary loves is a retired school teacher.
　　　　　　　　受　　　主　　動
瑪麗所愛的公車司機是一位退休的教師。

在例句中,我們用形容詞子句 whom Mary loves 來形容前面的主詞 The bus driver,由於在形容詞子句中瑪麗是主詞,而她所愛的人為受詞,所以用受格的關係代名詞 whom 來代替。

★3-1-1 限定和非限定形容詞子句

形容詞子句根據其前面的名詞（人、事、物）的性質或閱讀大眾對其了解與否，可分為限定形容詞子句和非限定形容詞子句。例句如下：

【非限定形容詞子句】

(1) Mary, who has two brothers, is my classmate.

有二位兄弟的瑪麗是我的同學。（瑪麗確實只有二位兄弟）

【限定形容詞子句】

(2) Mary who has two brothers is my classmate.

有二位兄弟的瑪麗是我的同學。（我們知道瑪麗有二位兄弟，但是她有幾位兄弟則不太曉得，可能是瑪麗只跟我提起這二位。）

非限定子句是在形容詞子句的前後用逗點來加以和主要子句分開。在例句(1)中，我們知道瑪麗確實只有二位兄弟，而且這是大家都知道的事實。限定子句則沒有用逗點和主要子句分開，在例句(2)中，我們不知道瑪麗到底有幾位兄弟（可能有四位或五位），但是她有提到這二位，所以我們僅能用二位來說明，同時保留補充說明的空間。再看下面的例句：

(1)非限定形容詞子句

The policemen, who received bribes from gangsters, abused their power.

收受流氓賄賂的警察濫用其權力。（暗指所有的警察都接受賄賂，都是壞人，而且大家都知道警察收賄的事實。）

(2)限定形容詞子句

The policemen who received bribes from gangsters abused their power.

只有收受流氓賄賂的警察濫用其權力。（只有收受賄賂的警察才是壞警察，濫用其權力，其他警察並沒有收受賄賂。）

在上述例句(1)中，我們用非限定形容詞子句來暗指所有的警察都接受流氓賄賂，而例句(2)中只有少數警察會接受賄賂。所以，在使用形容詞子句時有沒有逗點（限定和非限定）非常重要，一定要慎重，千萬不要犯了一竿子打翻一船人的嚴重錯誤。在《經濟學人》文章中所報導的人物、公司行號、產品、書、電影或是事件，都是大家平常耳熟能詳的新聞事件，因此都是採用非限定形容詞子句的寫作方式，例如：

Intel Corp., which is a leading chipmaker, announced higher than expected third quarter sales revenue report.

頂尖的電腦晶片製造商英特爾宣布高於預期的第三季營業額報告。

在例句中，大家都知道 Intel Co. 是全球知名的電腦晶片製造商，所以用非限定形容詞子句來補充說明其公司產業背景。

★3-1-2同位語

在非限定形容詞子句中常用到關係代名詞和其相關的動詞，整篇文章讀起來都是關係代名詞，不僅造成讀者閱讀困擾，同時造成贅字太多，占據過多版面空間的問題，為了解決這個問題，我們可使用同位語來取代非限定形容詞子句。

同位語顧名思義就是與其要形容的名詞是一體二面，也就是將非限定形容詞子句中的關係代名詞和動詞去掉，只留下受詞，就變成同位語了，其句型結構如下：

主詞，<u>關係代名詞＋動詞＋受詞</u>，＋動詞＋受詞
　　　　　　　形容詞子句
　　　　　　　↓
主詞，<u>受詞</u>，＋動詞＋受詞
　　　同位語

我們看以下的例句：

(1) Intel Corp., which is a leading chipmaker, announced higher than expected third quarter sales revenue report.

(2) Inter Corp., a leading chipmaker, announced higher than expected third quarter sales revenue report.

頂尖的電腦晶片製造商英特爾宣布高於預期的第三季營業報告。

在上述的例句中，我們將例句(1)中非限定形容詞子句中的關係代名詞 which 和動詞 is 去掉之後，將其受詞 a leading chipmaker 改成 a leading chipmaker 便成為同位語，如例句(2)中所示。例句(1)和例句(2)意思完全一

樣，但是例句(2)顯然比例句(1)來得更加簡潔有力了。我們再看下列的例句：

(1) Lee Kuan Yen, who is the founding father of Singapore, represents the old generation of Asian leaders who enjoy higher social status in the countries.

(2) Lee Kuan Yen, the founding father of Singapore, represents the old generation of Asian leaders who enjoy higher social status in the countries.

新加坡國父李光耀代表舊時代的亞洲領導者，他們在這些國家中擁有比較高的社會地位。

在上述例句中，我們將例句(1)中的非限定形容詞子句的關係代名詞 who 和動詞 is 去掉，保留受詞 the founding father of Singapore，就成為例句(2)中的同位語，成為例句(2)的結構。值得注意的是，例句(1)中的限定形容詞子句 who enjoy higher social status in the countries，由於不是非限定的用法，所以不能改為同位語，因為我們不知道這些國家的領導人是誰，句子中也沒有加以說明，所以只能用限定的形容詞子句。

3-1 練習

▶ 將下列二個句子中的形容詞子句或簡單句改寫成同位語。

1. Hewlett-Packard (HP) is a leader in laser printer manufacture. It has more than 6,000 employees in 20 countries.

2. Hamas would like to receive financial and humantain supports from any parties.
   Hamas is the radical Islamic group which rules the Gaza Strip.

3. General David Petraeus decides to support President Obama's decision to withdraw troops from Afghanistan.
   General Petraeus is the American commander of NATO's force.

4. Will Dudley, who is the president of New York Federal Reserve Bank, prefers "Quantitative Easing (QE)" monetary policy.

5. Johnson & Johnson has reached its 2020 CO_2 reduction target. It is one of the leading pharmaceutical companies in the world.

6. Android, which is an operating system for smartphone, is developed and marketed by Google.

7. Anna Chapman was arrested and departed by the State Department of America.
   She was a Russia's spy responsible for spying American nuclear facilities.

8. Peter Diamandis founded the X Prize Foundation to prompt the innovation in space aviation. He is the Chief Executive Officer (CEO) and co-founder of Zero Gravity Corp.

9. Dilma Rousseff and Jose Serra will face a run-off presidential election on October 31st, 2010. Ms. Rousseff is the chosen candidate of Brazilian President Luis Inacio Lula da silva.

10. Bill Clinton held a political rally in Los Angeles in support of Democratic candidates in the coming November mid-term election. Mr. Clinton is a former president of the United States.

📖 3-1 解答

1. *Hewlett-Packard (HP) , a leader in laser printer manufacture, has more than 6,000 employees in 20 countries.*
   中譯：雷射印表機的領先製造商惠普在全球 20 個國家中，擁有超過 6,000 位的員工。

2. *Hamas, the radical Islamic group which rules the Gaza Strip, would like to receive financial and humantain supports from any parties.*
   中譯：伊斯蘭激進團體同時控制加薩走廊的哈瑪斯，願意接受任何團體的金錢和人道支援。

3. *General David Petraeus, the American commander of NATO's force, decides to support President Obama's decision to withdraw troops from Afghanistan.*
   中譯：美軍北大西洋公約組織指揮官皮特魯將軍決定支持歐巴馬總統從阿富汗撤軍的決策。

4. *Will Dudley, the president of New York Federal Reserve Bank, prefers "Quantitative Easing (QE)" monetary policy.*
   中譯：紐約聯邦儲備銀行總裁戴利偏好「量化寬鬆」的貨幣政策。

5. *Johnson & Johnson, one of the leading pharmaceutical companies in the world, has reached its 2020 CO_2 reduction target.*
   中譯：頂尖製藥廠之一的嬌生公司已經達成其 2020 年二氧化碳減量目標。

6. *Android, an operating system for smartphone, is developed and marketed by Google.*
   中譯：智慧型手機作業系統 Android 是由 Google 開發和行銷。

7. *Anna Chapman, a Russia's spy responsible for spying American nuclear facilities, was arrested and departed by the State Department of America.*
   中譯：負責偵探美國核子設施的俄羅斯間諜安娜‧查普曼被美國國務院逮捕同時驅逐出境。

8. *Peter Diamandis, the Chief Executive Officer (CEO) and co-founder of Zero Gravity Corp., founded the X Prize Foundation to prompt the innovation in space aviation.*

中譯：零動公司執行長和共同創辦人的彼得‧戴蒙斯成立 X 大獎基金會來推動航空產業的創新發明。

9. *Dima Rousseff, the chosen candidate of Brazilian President Luis Inacio Lula da silva, and Jose Serra will face a run-off presidential election on October 31st, 2010.*

中譯：巴西總統魯拉選定的接班候選人迪瑪‧魯撤英和荷西‧西拉在 2010 年 10 月 31 日將面臨第二輪的總統選舉投票。

10. *Bill Clinton, a former president of the United States, held a political rally in Los Angeles in support of Democratic candidates in the coming November mid-term election.*

中譯：美國前總統柯林頓在洛山磯舉辦造勢大會，支持在 11 月期中選舉參選的民主黨候選人。

■3.2 名詞子句

★3-2-1 that 名詞子句

名詞子句顧名思義就是以句子的結構方式（主詞＋動詞＋受詞）成為名詞，在句子中作為主詞或受詞之用，名詞子句作為句子的主詞，強調事件的主體，名詞子句作為句子的受詞，表示對此事件的補充說明，名詞子句最典型的句子為用連接詞 that 所代表的名詞子句，其結構如下：

主1＋動1＋that＋主2＋動2＋受2
從屬子句

我們來看下面的例句：

President Obama said that he would ask both senators and
主1　　　動1　連接詞 主2　動2　　　　　受2
house representatives to pass the national health insurance plan.

歐巴馬總統請求參議員和眾議員通過全民健康保險計畫。

在上述例句中，主要子句中的主詞為 President Obama，動詞為 said，而受詞為 that he would ask both senators and house representatives to pass the national health insurance plan，我們稱 that 所接的子句為名詞子句，因為我們知道在主要子句中有主詞 President Obama 和動詞 said，而受詞就是 that 所接的子句，而受詞必須是名詞，所以 that 所接的子句，我們就簡稱為名詞子句。

一般來說，在句子中只要看到 that 就可直接判定是名詞子句，作為主要子句的受詞，而整個句子的其中文意義就是主詞要做（說／知道／明瞭／想／看）下列的事情，這件事情就用名詞子句來說明或做代表，主要子句配合名詞子句使用時，主要子句常用的動詞如下：

主詞1＋{ • agree • forget • see • ask
• hear • tell • believe • know ＋that＋主2＋動2＋受2
• think • find • say • understand }

例如：

Mr. Lin believed that he would pass the driver's licence test.
林先生相信他會通過汽車駕照考試。
或是林先生相信一件事，這件事就是他會通過汽車駕照考試。

★3-2-2 wh 名詞子句

名詞子句除了有上述 that 所代表的名詞子句之外，另外就是由 wh (what, when, why, whether) 所代表的名詞子句。

我們先看下面的例句：

The TV program which you watched yesterday **was very**
　　　主1　　　　　　　　　形容詞子句　　　　　　動1

interesting.
受1

昨天晚上你所看的電視節目非常有趣。

在句子中，我們用形容詞子句 which you watched yesterday 來形容前面的主詞 The TV program。上述的句子，就是我們在第三章第一節所討論的形容詞子句或是複雜句的句型結構，但是我們可以用 wh 的名詞子句將形容詞子句加以改寫，如下：

What you watched yesterday was very interesting.
　　名詞子句當主詞　　　　　　動詞　　　受詞

昨天你所看的非常有趣。

在例句中動詞是 was，受詞是 very interesting，但是少了主詞。我們知道動詞 was 的前面要擺主詞，What you watched yesterday 雖然是間接疑問句的結構，但是已經成為句子中的主詞，而主詞必須為名詞，所以我們將 What you watched yesterday 稱為名詞子句，在中文的翻譯上 wh 的名詞子句我們通常翻譯為（……東西）、（所說過的話……）、（……所做的事情……）、和（……的意思）、（如何做……）以及（為什麼……）。我們看下面的例句：

(1) Mexico's drug-related violence has spreaded to its northern neighbor, the United States.

(2) What makes Americans worrying is not only the rising violence crime numbers but also the increasing drug cartel power.

墨西哥和販毒有關的暴力犯罪已經擴散到其北邊的國家，美國。令美國人擔心的不僅是不斷上升的犯罪數據，而且還包括增加的販毒卡特爾組織的影響力。

在例句(1)中，我們指出墨西哥與販毒有關的暴力犯罪不斷擴散到其北邊國家美國，而在例句(2)中名詞子句 what makes Americans worrying 來代表例句(1)的意思，而後才用動詞 is 和受詞 not only the rising violence crime numbers but also the increasing drug cartel power 來完成這個句子的結構。

接下來介紹用 whether~or（是否）所組成的名詞子句：

Tim Pawlenty, governor of Minnesota, insistes that states have

名詞子句1

the final say to decide **whether they want to implement the**

名詞子句2

national health plan quickly or slowly.

明尼蘇達州州長提姆‧包瓦提堅持州政府有權決定是否要立即或延後執行全國健保計畫。

在上述例句中，我們用名詞子句 whether they want to implement the national health plan quickly or slowly 來當作 decide 的受詞。在上述的例句中，呈現了同位語，governor of Minnesota 來形容主詞 Tim Pawlenty，接著用動詞 insistes，而後接 that 的名詞子句 that states have the final say to decide，之後再根據名詞子句1的動詞 decide 接名詞子句2 whether they want to implement the national health plan quickly or slowly，這種句型為典型的《經濟學人》英文句型結構。

3-2 練習

▶ 找出下列句子中的名詞子句。

1. China has insisted that Taiwan is one of its core interests in Sino-American foreign policy agenda.

2. As a rule of thumb, modern economics clearly states that a rich nation produces rich goods which includes military equipments and aviation crafts.

3. President Dmitry Medvedev promised that the new science park in Skolkovo, Russia's answer to Silicon Valley, had the human capital and government-supported fund to succeed in the future.

4. It is impossible that China may raise its interest rate in the near term to cool the overheated economy.

5. Whether the Democratic Party or the Republican Party will control the House of Representatives and the Senate after the mid-term election is an unsolved problem now.

6. Standard Chartered Bank, a Britain's bank, announced that it would raise £3.0 billion in a seasonal rights issue.

7. Why unemployment remained at 10% despite government's $50 billion stimulus package puzzled many politicians and government officials.

8. U.S. Treasury Secretary Tim Geithner said that China's lax monetary policy would jeopardize the world's fragile recovering economy.

9. When Jacob Zuma came to power in 2009, President Zuma promised that human rights would guide South Africa foreign affairs.

10. President Nicolas Sarkozy and Prime Minister David Cameron will attend the bilateral summit and state that two countries will strength their NATO roles.

📖3-2 解答

1. *that Taiwan is one of its core interests in Sino-American foreign policy agenda*
   中譯：中國堅持臺灣是中美外交政策議題中的重要議案之一。

2. *that a rich nation produces rich goods which includes military equipments and aviation crafts*
   中譯：根據經驗法則，現代經濟學清楚的表明富有國家生產包括軍事設備和航太船艦的先進商品。

3. *that the new science park in Skolkovo, Russia's answer to Silicon Valley, had the human capital and government-supported fund to succeed in the future*
   中譯：梅帝弟總統承諾媲美美國矽谷的斯科科夫科學園區，有人力資源和政府支持的資金，能在將來成功。

4. *that China may raise its interest rate in the near term to cool the overheated economy*
   中譯：中國在不久的將來不可能調高利率，以冷卻過熱的經濟發展。

5. *Whether the Democratic Party or the Republican Party will control the House of Representatives and the Senate after the mid-term election*
   中譯：民主黨或是共和黨在期中選舉後是否掌控美國國會，到目前為止是一個未解的難題。

6. *that it would raise £3.0 billion in a seasonal rights issue*
   中譯：英國的渣打銀行宣布將現金增資發行新股，募資 30 億英鎊。

7. *Why unemployment remained at 10% despite government's $50 billion stimulus package*
   中譯：在政府 500 億美元的刺激方案之後，失業率仍然停留在 10%，令許多民意代表和政府官員感到困惑。

8. *that China's lax monetary policy would jeopardize the world's fragile recovering economy*
   中譯：美國財政部長蓋特納表示，中國寬鬆的貨幣政策可能危害脆弱又正在復甦的世界經濟。

9. *that human rights would guide South Africa foreign affairs*
　中譯：當祖馬在 2009 年當選南非總統時，承諾人
　　　　權將主導南非的外交事務。

10. *that two countries will strength their NATO roles*
　中譯：法國總統薩柯琪和英國首相喀麥隆將參加雙
　　　　邊高峰會，同時表明二國將強化在北大西
　　　　洋公約組織的角色。

■3.3 副詞子句

在上述形容詞子句和名詞子句的例句中，我們可以從句子中主詞或受詞的結構中，清楚的看出這是形容詞子句，或是名詞子句。例如形容詞子句（同位語）常擺在主詞或受詞後面，來形容前面的主詞或受詞，例句如下：

(1) Dmitry Medvedev, who is Russia's president, asked

    主詞   形容詞子句

Moscow mayor Yuri Luzhkov to step down.

俄羅斯總統梅帝弟要求莫斯科市長魯科夫辭職下臺。

(2) Russia's Prime Minister Vladimir Putin has suggested Sergei Sobyanin, who is the ruling elite of Russia, as mayor of

  受詞   形容詞子句

Moscow.

俄羅斯總理浦亭建議俄羅斯統治精英沙巴尼出任莫斯科市長。

或是名詞子句用來說明某事件，例如：

Hillary Clinton, the American secretary of state, states that Britain is the most capable partner of American force in the

        名詞子句

Middle East.

美國國務卿希拉蕊表示英國是美國在中東最有力的夥伴。

但是副詞子句在區分上就顯得比較困難，副詞子句用來修飾句子中的動詞、副詞、形容詞或整個句子，通常用來表示條件、時間、地點、原因或結果的修飾，例如：

If Iran acquired a nuclear capability, Israel would bomb

    副詞子句   主要子句

Tehran, the capital city of Iran, immediately.

如果伊朗具備製造核子武器的能力時，以色列將立即轟炸伊朗首都德黑蘭。

在上述的句子中,我們用主要子句 Israel would bomb Tehran, the capital city of Iran,表示全句的意思,但是用條件副詞子句 If Iran acquired a nuclear capacity 來說明主要子句要實行的前提條件。

一般來說,副詞子句常用的詞語如表3-3所示。

表3-3

因果關係	時間關係	讓步關係	條件句關係	比較關係
since as because	before after while when	although even though	if unless in case	比較級more~than as~as

而《經濟學人》常用的副詞子句為讓步關係的 although 和 even though,條件句關係的 if 和 unless,或是比較關係的 more-than,例如:

Although Chile's 33 trapped miners have been rescued, the
從屬子句(副詞子句)

reform of Codelco, the state-owned copper company is a long
主要子句

way to go.

雖然 33 名受困的智利礦工已被救出,但是整頓國營的科頓科銅礦公司還有很長的一段路要走。

在主要子句中,主詞是 the reform of Codelco,而且用同位語 the state-owned copper company 來說明 Codelco 這家公司的背景,而後用動詞 is 和受詞 a long way to go 來完成句子,而副詞子句(從屬子句)只是用來針對 Codelco 這家公司需要改革的補充說明,雖然它是副詞子句,但還是有主詞、有動詞的句子結構,主詞 Chile's 33 trapped miners,動詞 have been rescued 來完成整個副詞子句。接下來,我們來看比較級的副詞子句:

According to a report published by Stephen Dorgan
形容詞片語

of Mckinsey, a management consulting firm, health-care
同位語　　　　　　　　　　　　　　　主詞

institutions that hire more qualified staff score better than those

<u>　　　　　　　　形容詞子句　　　　　動詞　　　　副詞子句</u>

that do not.

　　根據麥肯錫管理顧問公司史帝芬‧道格的報告，僱用較多合格員工的醫療機構得分高於那些沒有較多合格員工的醫療機構。

　　在上述的例句中，主詞是 health-care institutions，動詞是 score，而副詞子句則是 better than those that do not。而其他的都是配角了，例如用形容詞片語 According to a report published by Stephen Dorgan of Mckinsey 來做整篇文章的開頭，同位語 a management consulting firm 則用來形容前面的 Mckinsey 做公司背景說明。另外一個形容詞子句 that hire more qualified staff 則用來形容前面的 institutions，做比較級主詞的背景說明。從以上的說明，我們可以知道一般《經濟學人》的文章中，通常都將形容詞子句、名詞子句和副詞子句變成從屬子句，配合主要子句做事件背景的說明或補充敘述。要看懂這些句子其實非常簡單，只要找出主要子句的主詞、動詞和受詞就是整篇句子的重點了，至於從屬子句（形容詞子句、名詞子句和副詞子句）看得懂或是看不懂就不重要了。例如，我們將上述的句子改寫成簡單句的結構就非常清楚了。

Stephen Dorgan of Mckinsey published a report. Mckinsey is a management consulting firm. Health-care institutions with more qualified staff score better than those health-care institutions with less qualified staff.

　　麥肯錫的史辛芬‧道格發表一篇報告，麥肯錫是一家管理顧問公司，僱用較多合格的員工之醫療機構，得分高於僱用較少合格員工的醫療機構。

3-3 練習

▶ 找出下列句子中的副詞子句。

1. When President Obama visited Indonesia in November 2010, Susilo Bambang Yudhoyono, President of Indonesia, discussed Indonesia's role at international stage with President Obama.

2. Although freedom of speech and freedom of press are enshrined in China's constitution, Chain continuously censors magazines, newspapers and internets.

3. Angela Merkel, Chancellor of Germany, keeps saying that the country is not a country of immigration even though the foreigners have reached 9% of the total population.

4. When the Organization of the Petroleum Exporting Countries (OPEC) implemented oil embargo in 1973, the oil crisis triggered the world's recession that lasted for 5 years.

5. Unless developed countries can find the substitute for fossil oil, petroleum-powered cars are still running around the roads.

6. If Terra Firma, an European private-equity firm, could roll again this time, EMI, a British music company, which Terra Firma bought for £4.0 billion in 2007, was one of the worst mergers and acquisitions (M&A) deals in 2007.

7. When Michael Milken was a student at the University of California, Berkeley, in the late 1960s, Mr. Milken build an empirical model which proved that high-yield bonds outperformed investment-grade bonds.

8. After Michael Milken was sentenced to 10 years in prison after pleading guilty of security fraud, Drexel Burnham Lambert, which was a major Wall Street investment bank, was forced into bankruptcy in February 1990.

9. When Drexel successfully helped Kohlberg Kravis Roberts (KKR), a buyout firm, to raise $25 billion in bond issue, many corporate raiders and leveraged buyout (LBO) firms started using junk bonds to finance their M&A deals.

10. Moet Hennessy Louis Vuitton(LVMH), the world's largest luxury-goods company based in Paris, France, reported a 30% increase of sales revenue, which was the biggest single year increase in the company's history even though the world was still in recession.

3-3 解答

1. *When President Obama visited Indonesia in November 2010*
   中譯：當歐巴馬總統在 2010 年 11 月訪問印尼時，印尼總統約多約諾和歐巴馬總統討論印尼在國際舞臺的角色。

2. *Although freedom of speech and freedom of press are enshrined in China's constitution*
   中譯：雖然中國憲法保障言論和出版自由，中國仍然不斷對雜誌、報紙和網路實施檢查。

3. *even though the foreigners have reached 9% of the total population*
   中譯：雖然移民人口已達到德國全國人口的 9%，德國總理梅克爾仍然不斷說明德國不是一個移民的國家。

4. *When the Organization of the Petroleum Exporting Countries (OPEC) implemented oil embargo in 1973*
   中譯：當石油輸出國組織在 1973 年實施石油禁運後，石油危機啟動了長達 5 年的世界經濟蕭條。

5. *Unless developed countries can find the substitute for fossil oil*
   中譯：除非已開發國家能找到石油替代品，否則石油驅動的汽車仍然會在大街小巷奔馳。

6. *If Terra Firma, an European private-equity firm, could roll again this time*
   中譯：如果法碼私募基金這次能夠再度發揮本能，否則 2007 年以 40 億英鎊購併英國音樂製作公司科藝百代可能是當年最差的購併交易之一。

7. *When Michael Milken was a student at the University of California, Berkeley, in the late 1960s.*

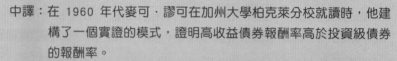

中譯：在 1960 年代麥可‧謬可在加州大學柏克萊分校就讀時，他建構了一個實證的模式，證明高收益債券報酬率高於投資級債券的報酬率。

8. *After Michael Milken was sentenced to 10 years in prison after pleading guilty of security fraud*

中譯：當麥可‧謬可因為證券詐欺罪被判刑 10 年後，華爾街重量級的投資銀行卓克索在 1990 年 2 月被迫申報破產。

9. *When Drexel successfully helped Kohlberg Kravis Roberts (KKR), a buyout firm, to raise $25 billion in bond issue*

中譯：當卓克索幫助購併企業 KKR 發行債券，募集 250 億美元，許多企業購併者和運用融資購併的企業開始發行垃圾債券，來募集資金進行購併交易。

10. *even though the world was still in recession*

中譯：雖然全球經濟仍然處於衰退，但是位在法國巴黎的全球最大奢侈品集團路易‧威登申報公司有史以來單一年度銷售額最大增幅，營業額收入增加高達 30%。

第三章 綜 合 練 習

▶ 請將下列文章中的形容詞子句、同位語、名詞子句、副詞子句全部
找出來。

Unless French President Nicolas Sarkozy backed down the pension reform, angry French workers would continuously blockade fuel refineries and Paris's streets, which cost the country $20 million dollars a day. Like France, many European countries are unprepared to face the coming retirement of baby boomers. Pension funds which are contributed by workers and corporations are running low at every European country. German's funds reached the historical lowest point. Chancellor Angela Merkel said that bringing more young people from Eastern Europe, for example Poland, Serbia and Bulgaria, would solve the problem. Germany companies have long history of recruiting guest workers from Southern Europe in the 1960s. Gerhard Schroder, Chancellor of Germany from 1998 to 2005, opened the gate for immigration and brought in more than 100,000 "guest workers" who were called by Germans. Young workers tend to be more productivity than those of aging ones. The new work force also increases the payment of pension contribution which is a defined-contribution plan in Germany. But many immigrants are reluctant to integrate into the society. The vision of multiculturalism which allows ethnic-based separate communities to live side by side happily has run into a deadlock. Even though the country has relax immigration requirements, Ilyas Musharraf, a 30-year-old Pakistan guest worker, says that he would not bring his family to Germany.

綜合練習

_____

_____

_____

_____

_____

_____

_____

_____

_____

▌第三章 綜合練習解答 ▌

★形容詞子句

which cost the country $20 million dollars a day

which are contributed by workers and corporations

who were called by Germans

which is a defined-contribution plan

which allows ethnic-based separate communities to live side by side happily

★同位語

Chancellor of Germany from 1998 to 2005

a 30-year-old Pakistan guest worker

★名詞子句

that bringing more young people from Eastern Europe, for example Poland, Serbia and Bulgaria, would solve the problem

that he would not bring his family to Germany

★副詞子句

more productivity than those of aging ones

Unless French President Nicolas Sarkozy backed down the pension reform

Even though the country has relax immigration requirements

第三章 單字

★The Tea Party Movement
茶黨運動

★organize 組織起來

★financial industry 金融產業

★retire 退休

★bribe 賄賂

★gangster 流氓

★abuse 濫用

★Intel Corp. 英特爾公司

★chipmaker 電腦晶片製造商

★third quarter 第三季

★sales revenue 營業額

★Lee Kuan Yen 李光耀

★founding father 國父

★Singapore 新加坡

★generation 世代

★Asian 亞洲的

★social 社會的

★status 地位

★Hewlett-Packard (HP) 惠普

★laser printer 雷射印表機

★manufacture 製造

★Hamas 哈瑪斯

★radical 激進的

★Islamic group 伊斯蘭團體

★the Gaza Strip 加薩走廊

★Afghanistan 阿富汗

★Commander 指揮官

★NATO 北大西洋公約組織

★force 部隊

★New York Fed
紐約聯邦準備銀行

★prefer 喜歡

★Quantitative Easing (QE)
量化寬鬆

★monetary policy 貨幣政策

★Johnson & Johnson 嬌生公司

★CO_2 (Carbon Dioxide) 二氧化碳

★operating system 作業系統

★arrest 逮捕

★depart 驅逐

★the State Department of
America 美國國務院

★spy 偵探

★responsible for 負責

★nuclear facilities 核子設施

★foundation 基金會

★innovation 創新發明

★aviation 航空

★co-founder 共同創辦人

★a run-off presidential election
第二輪總統選舉

★candidate 候選人

★Brazilian President Luis Inacio
Lula da silva 巴西總統魯拉

★a political rally 選舉造勢大會

★Democratic candidates
民主黨候選人

★mid-term election 期中選舉

★former president 前總統

★senator 參議員

★house representative 眾議員

★pass 通過

★the national health insurance plan 全民健保計畫

★drug-related violence 和販毒有關的暴力犯罪

★spread 擴散

★drug cartel 販毒卡特爾組織

★final say 最後決定權

★implement 執行

★Sino-American 中美

★agenda 議題

★a rule of thumb 經驗法則

★crafts 船或飛機

★aviation 航太

★military 軍事

★human capital 人力資本（源）

★government-supported fund 政府支持的基金

★Silicon Valley 矽谷

★near term 最近

★overheated economy 過熱的經濟發展

★the Democratic Party 民主黨

★the Republican Party 共和黨

★an unsolved problem 未解的難題

★Standard Chartered Bank 渣打銀行

★a seasonal rights issue 現金增資發行新股

★unemployment 失業（率）

★remain 保留、停留

★stimulus package 刺激方案

★puzzle 困惑

★politicians 政客或民意代表

★government official 政府官員

★Treasury Secretary 財政部長

★lax 寬鬆的

★jeopardize 危害

★fragile 破碎的、脆弱的

★recovering economy 復甦的經濟

★President Zuma 南非總統祖馬

★human rights 人權

★foreign affairs 外交事務

★President Nicolas Sarkozy 法國總統薩柯琪

★Prime Minister David Cameron 英國首相喀麥隆

★the bilateral summit 雙邊高峰會

★strength 強化

★roles 角色

★ruling elite 統治精英

★the Middle East 中東

★Iran 伊朗

★nuclear capability
核子武器能力

★bomb 轟炸

★Tehran 德黑蘭，伊朗首都

★trapped 受困的

★miner 礦工

★rescue 拯救

★reform 整頓、改革

★state-owned 國營的

★copper 銅礦

★Mckinsey 麥肯錫顧問公司

★a management consulting firm
一間管理顧問公司

★health-care 醫療保健

★institutions 法人機構

★qualified staff 合格的員工
（有相關證照的員工）

★score 得分

★Indonesia 印尼

★discuess 討論

★stage 舞臺

★freedom of speech 言論自由

★freedom of press 出版自由

★enshrine 書寫、供奉、保障

★constitution 憲法

★continuously 不斷的、持續的

★censor 檢查

★Angela Merkel 梅克爾

★Chancellor of Germany
德國總理

★immigration 移民

★population 人口

★Organization of the
Petroleum Exporting Countries
(OPEC)
石油輸出國組織

★implement 執行

★oil embargo 石油禁運

★oil crisis 石油危機

★trigger 啟動

★recession 蕭條

★developed countries
已開發國家

★substitute 替代品

★fossil oil 原油

★petroleum-powered cars
石油驅動的汽車

★a private-equity firm 私募基金

★EMI 科藝百代公司

★mergers and acquisitions (M&A)
購併

★the University of California,
Berkeley 加州大學柏克萊分校

★1960s 1960年代

★an empirical model 實證模式

★high-yield bonds 高收益債券

★investment-grade bonds
投資級債券

★bond 債券

★sentence 判刑

★pleading 承認
★guilty 有罪
★security fraud 證券詐欺
★Wall Street 華爾街
★investment bank 投資銀行
★forced 被迫
★bankruptcy 破產
★a buy out firm 一家購併企業
★bond issue 發行債券
★raise 募集
★corporate raiders 企業購併者
★leveraged buyout (LBO) firms 運用融資購併的企業
★junk bonds 垃圾債券
★finance 資助
★M&A deals 購併交易
★Moet Hennessy Louis Vuitton (LVMH) 路易‧威登集團
★luxury-goods 奢侈品
★sales revenue 營業額
★backed down 撤回
★blockade 阻擋
★fuel refineries 石油煉製廠
★unprepare 沒有準備好
★retirement 退休
★baby boomers 二戰後出生嬰兒潮
★pension funds 退休基金
★contribute 貢獻
★historical 歷史性的

★chancellor 總理
★Eastern Europe 東歐
★Poland 波蘭
★Serbia 塞爾亞
★Bulgaria 保加利亞
★recruit 招募
★guest workers 外籍勞工
★productivity 生產力
★aging ones 年老的勞工
★defined-contribution 定額提撥
★reluctant 不願意
★integrate 整合、合併
★multiculturalism 多元文化主義
★ethnic-based 以種族為基礎的
★communities 社區
★a deadlock 進退不得
★Pakistan 巴基斯坦

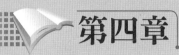

第四章 分詞、分詞片語和分詞構句

在第一章八大詞類我們曾經討論過形容詞擺在名詞前面,用以形容後面的名詞,增加句子的可看性和閱讀的樂趣,也可以看出寫作者對於用字遣詞的功力,例如:

(1) Mary Lin is a girl.

林瑪麗是一位女孩。

(2) Mary Lin is a beautiful girl.

林瑪麗是一位美麗的女孩。

很顯然的在例句(2)中的受詞 girl ,前面加入形容詞 beautiful 之後,整個句子就有了畫龍點睛之效了。但是英文中的形容詞卻是有限的,為了增加形容詞的數量,便有變通的方法,也就是分詞當作形容詞來使用。

■4.1 分詞前位修飾

分詞就是動詞字尾加 ing 或 ed 成為現在分詞和過去分詞，而現在分詞或是過去分詞所代表的意義卻大不同。一般來說，分詞所代表的意義如表4-1。

表4-1

分詞	形態	意義	單字
現在分詞	Ving	進行中	developing
過去分詞	Ved	已完成	developed

分詞前位修飾的意思代表分詞是擺在被修飾名詞的前面，符合一般的寫作習慣，分詞當形容詞時，只有一個分詞單字時擺在名詞前面，作為前位修飾，當分詞後面接其他單字時，形成二個字以上的分詞片語，擺在名詞的後面形成後位修飾。

★4-1-1現在分詞

現在分詞就是一般動詞字尾加上 ing ，代表正在進行中動作或主動的意義，例如：

Taiwan is a developing country.

分詞＝形容詞

臺灣是一個開發中國家。

在上述的例句中，其實是一個簡單句 Taiwan is a country.。但是為了表示臺灣經濟發展的程度，我們用開發的原形動詞 develop 加上 ing 變成現在分詞 developing，擺在名詞（受詞）前面成為形容詞，便成為加上現在分詞的句子。

為什麼現在分詞代表進行中的意思呢，其實我們如果回想現在進行式的句子架構，便知道其中的道理。

現在進行式：主詞＋be 動詞＋一般動詞現在分詞＋受詞

Taiwanese people are developing their country.

動詞　現在分詞

臺灣人正在開發其國家。

上述的句子正是現在進行式的例句，因為用了 developing 這個現在進行式的現在分詞，因此可將此字當作分詞視同形容詞，擺在名詞（受詞）前面，便成為 Taiwan is a developing country. 的例句了。

如果我們用形容詞子句來說明的話，就不難了解分詞（開發中）其中的意義。例如：

Taiwan is a country which is been developing now.

形容詞子句

臺灣是一個國家，她正在被開發中。

在上述的例句中，我們用形容詞子句 which is been developing now 來形容其前面的名詞（受詞）country，但是我們運用形容詞子句共四個單字來形容 country 這個字，如果我們只用一個單字 developing 來形容 country，那很顯然的我們寫作的功力就相差很多了，畢竟用字精簡不囉嗦，正是英文寫作修辭的重心。這也是為什麼在《經濟學人》的文章中，常用同位語和現在分詞來取代形容詞子句的原因了。

★4-1-2過去分詞

過去分詞則代表已完成或被動的意思。

首先我們來看已完成的句子結構，例句如下：

The United States is a developed country.

分詞＝形容詞

美國是一個已開發國家。

同樣的，上述是一個簡單句 The United States is a country.，但是為了表示美國是一個經濟高度開發的國家，民眾享有高度的生活水準，我們用開發的原形動詞 develop 的過去分詞 developed 擺在名詞（受詞）前面，成為形容詞，便成為加上過去分詞的句子了。

為什麼用過去分詞代表已完成的意思呢？我們將完成式句子結構表示出來，便知道其中的道理：

現在完成式：主詞＋have(has)＋一般動詞過去分詞＋受詞

Americans have developed their country.

美國人已完成開發其國家。

上述的例句是現在完成式的句子，代表現在已完成，並且持續下去的狀態，因為用了 developed 的過去分詞，因此可將本字當作分詞視為形容詞，擺在名詞（受詞）前面，便成為 The United States is a developed country. 的例句了。

我們曾經說過，過去分詞可以改寫成形容詞子句，例句如下：

The United States is a country which has been developed.

形容詞子句

美國是一個國家，她已被開發。

在上述例句中，我們用形容詞子句 which has been developed 來形容前面的名詞（受詞）country。

我們曾說過去分詞有被動的意思，我們用下列的句子來說明：

The stolen bike was found by the police.

分詞＝形容詞

被偷的腳踏車被警察找到了。

在上述的例句中，我們用過去分詞 stolen 來形容名詞（主詞）bike，腳踏車不可能自己遺失，一定是被偷（被動），因此分詞 stolen 有被動的意思，其實原句是用被動的形容詞子句所構成，例句如下：

The bike which was stolen was found by the police.

形容詞子句

被偷的腳踏車被警察找到了。

在例句中，我們用形容詞子句 which was stolen 來形容前面的名詞（主詞）bike，但是如果能用 stolen 一個字來代表整個形容詞子句三個單字的話，很顯然用過去分詞在寫作上更佳了。

現在分詞代表進行中的意思，而過去分詞代表已完成的意思，如果熟悉分詞的用法，就可知道其中的奧妙，而會心一笑了，請看下面的例句：

(1) The memorial service of Michael Jackson, a fallen star, was held on July 7th, 2009, at the Staples Center in Los Angeles, California.

已去世的明星麥克‧傑克森的喪禮，於 2009 年 7 月 7 日在加州洛杉磯史坦伯中心舉行。

(2) Paris Hilton, a falling star, represents the modern phenomenon of celebrities, who are prompted by tabloid magazines and paparazzi.

逐漸褪色的明星芭麗絲‧希爾頓，代表由八卦雜誌和狗仔隊所鼓吹的現代名人現象。

在例句(1)中，用代表已完成的過去分詞 a fallen star 表示已殞落的麥可‧傑克森，因為麥可本人已經去世，不可能再復出演藝圈。而在例句(2)中，我們用進行中的現在分詞 a falling star 代表芭麗絲的演藝事業逐漸走下坡，但不是已經完全結束，如果芭麗絲稍微改變行事風格或增強歌藝，或許還能東山再起。從以上二種分詞的用法就可看出寫作人在運用分詞（現在分詞和過去分詞）當作形容詞來形容後面的名詞時，對這事或這人的看法了。

★以下就是《經濟學人》常用的分詞

現在分詞		過去分詞	
英	中	英	中
the ruling party	執政黨	unmarried lovers	沒有婚約的戀人
pressing issues	急迫性的議題	registered users	已註冊會員
galling truth	令人困擾難以釋懷的真相	polluted farms	受污染的農地
existing concession	現有的讓步（妥協）	blocked internet services	被封鎖的網際網路
gathering storm	風雨來襲	undivided control	未分裂的控制
striking stories	震驚的事件	detailed plan	詳細的計畫
busting industry	衰退的產業	advanced degree	高階的學位
managing director	常務董事	advanced technology	高科技
growing number	逐漸增加的數量	diminished appeal	已退燒的訴求
rising star	如日中天的明星	seasoned boss	有經驗的老闆
declining country	衰退中的國家	respected figures	令人尊敬的人物
aging society	老人化的社會	failed referendum	失敗的公投
leading producer	領先的廠商（企業）	listed company	股票上市公司
remaining taboo	現存的禁忌	desired result	預期的結果
starring player	先發球員	known truth	已知的真相
starting actor	領銜主演男演員	uncharted territory	未知的領域
supporting actor	男配角	uncharted water	未知的領域
running water	自來水	noted scholar	知名的學者
failing state	失敗的政府（治理功能失敗的政府）	integrated world	整合的世界
booming economy	繁榮的經濟	talented students	有天分的學生
leading position	領先的位置	satisfied customer	滿意的顧客

現在分詞		過去分詞	
英	中	英	中
rating agency	評比單位	limited access	有限的通路
emerging economies	新興國家	unexpected benefit	預料外的好處
driving force	驅動力	expected result	預料中的結果
processing power	處理能力	disputed island	有爭議的島域
following year	明年	estimated result	預期的後果
living ones	倖存者	unreported story	未報導的故事
alarming event	警示（威脅）的事件	complicated issue	複雜的問題
existing applications	現有的應用軟體	spoiled boy	被寵壞的男孩
underlying truth	事實的真相	spilt milk	覆水
		organized crime	組織犯罪
		contaminated water	受污染的飲用水
		undervalued currency	被低估的貨幣
		overvalued currency	被高估的貨幣
		experienced politicians	有經驗的政治家
		mixed fortune	錯綜複雜的結果
		armed force	軍事武力
		retired army	已退休的軍人
		gated community	封閉有保全的社區
		sophisticated system	精密的系統
		detailed plan	詳細的計畫
		scheduled plan	已安排的計畫
		unsolved problem	未解的難題

▶ 找出下列句子中的分詞。

1. Although the mid-term election results will be know until on November 2nd, 2010, a gathering storm is clouded on the Capitol Hill.

2. Many registered internet users can not access their favour sites. The blocked Twitter service has issued a complain to Chinese government.

3. The galling truth is that Indonesia, which is responsible for "Haze" pollution, doesn't reach a general agreement with its tribal people. Air pollution indexes in south Malaysian peninsula and Singapore have reached alarming levels.

4. China's unreliable statistics, which didn't take into account of unreported bonus, complicated property deals and unknown shady gifts, has showed that its GDP per capital was $3,200 in 2009.

5. Foreign students who earned advanced degrees in maths, engineering and computer science have difficulty in getting H-1B Visas. Skilled foreign workers from Mexico are having the same problem.

6. Although known terrorists' photographs have posted on the London Heathrow Airport, armed policemen are scanning passengers one by one after the terrorist attack alarm had been issued.

7. Many talented staff in IBM, a computer software firm, have participated in "Giving a Day" volunteering work in Ho Chi Minh City, Vietnam. The program, which was called the Peace Corp of Corporation was launched in 2007 by Sam Palmisano, IBM' s chief executive.

8. Word of mouth is the proven marketing strategy even in the era of social networking.

9. When the stock market's free fall reached its height in 2008, an estimated 80 percent of retirement-saving accounts, which was known as 401k, suffered tremendous losses.

10. Disqualified homeowners, who can't access Treasury Department's mortgage-modification program, saw their home values under water by 50 percent.

4-1 解答

1. *gathering*
   中譯：就算期中選舉的結果要到 2010 年 11 月 2 日才能揭曉，國會山莊已經山雨欲來風滿樓。

2. *registered, blocked*
   中譯：許多已註冊的網際網路會員，無法連線到他們喜歡的網站，被封鎖的推特發出一封抱怨信給中國政府。

3. *galling, alarming*
   中譯：令人難以釋懷的真相是造成霾害的元凶，印尼政府無法和其原住民達成協議，馬來半島南部和新加坡的空氣污染指標已經達到警戒水準。

4. *unreported, complicated, unknown*
   中譯：沒將未申報的紅利、複雜的土地交易，和不可知祕密的禮物等納入統計的不可靠的中國統計數字顯示，在 2009 年中國每人國內生產毛額為美元 3,200 元。

5. *advanced, skilled*
   中譯：擁有數學、工程和電腦科技高階學歷的外國學生很難取得 H-1B 簽證，來自墨西哥的技術工人也面臨相同的問題。

6. *known, armed*
   中譯：雖然已知恐怖分子的相片已張貼在倫敦希斯洛機場，在恐怖分子攻擊的警報發布後，武裝警察針對旅客一一檢查。

7. *talented, volunteering*
   中譯：電腦軟體公司 IBM 內許多有才能的員工在越南胡志明市參與「奉獻一天」的志工活動，被稱為企業和平志工團的「奉獻一天」計畫，是在 2007 年由 IBM 總裁山姆‧潘密斯諾所發起的。

8. *proven*
   中譯：就算是在社群網的時代，口碑仍然是證明有效的行銷策略。

9. *estimated*
   中譯：當股票市場 2008 年重挫到最低點時，有 80% 的被稱之 401k 的退休儲蓄帳戶，都蒙受重大的損失。

10. *disqualified*
    中譯：無法符合財政部房地產貸款修正計畫資格的屋主，眼見她們房地產價值下跌 50%。

■4.2 分詞片語

分詞片語稱之為片語，代表它是由二個以上的單字來組成，其中第一個單字是分詞，所以稱之為分詞片語。

分詞片語後位修飾的意思，代表我們將分詞片語擺在要形容的名詞後面，形成從後面位置來形容前面的句子結構，其句型結構如下：

主詞＋分詞片語＋動詞＋受詞

從分詞片語後位修飾的方式更能突顯現在分詞代表主動的意思，而過去分詞代表被動的意思，我們首先來討論現在分詞片語後位修飾的例句。

(1) John walking in the woods finds a wounded bear.

分詞片語＝形容詞

走在森林中的約翰發現一隻受傷的熊。

在例句中，我們用分詞片語 walking in the woods 從後面來形容名詞（主詞）John，而且是用現在分詞 walking 來代表 John 自己主動走在森林中。 我們曾經說過分詞就是形容詞子句的簡寫，如果將分詞片語寫成複雜句中形容詞子句的話，就不難看出為何現在分詞代表主動的意思了，例句如下：

John who walks in the woods finds a wounded bear.

形容詞子句

走在森林中的約翰發現一隻受傷的熊。

在上述的例句中，我們用限定的形容詞子句 who walks in the woods 來形容前面的名詞（主詞）John，這是傳統複雜句的寫作，但是在能省則省的精簡英文要求下，可以把關係代名詞 who 省略，形成下列的句子：

John walking in the woods finds a wounded bear.

如果把 who 去掉，則整個句子有二個動詞 walks 和 finds，但是真正的動詞是主要子句 John finds a wounded bear 中的 finds，此時只能把形容詞子句中的 walks 改為現在分詞 walking，而且在形容詞子句中是 John 自己走在森林中 who walks in the woods，不是被迫（被動）走在森林中 who is walked in the woods。所以用現在分詞 walking 代表是 John 自己主動的意思，現在分詞 walking 有主動的味道。我們將限定形容詞子句改寫成分詞片語後位修飾的例句再複習一遍。

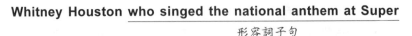

Whitney Houston who singed the national anthem at Super

形容詞子句

Bowl XXV in January 1991 was arrested for possession of marijuana at an airport.

Whitney Houston singing the national anthem at Super Bowl

分詞片語

XXV in January 1991 was arrested for possession of marijuana at an airport.

曾經在 1991 年 1 月第 25 屆超級杯演唱美國國歌的惠妮・休斯頓因持有大麻在機場被捕。

接下來再看有被動意思的過去分詞片語，如何從後位修飾前面的名詞，例句如下：

The book written by John is the best-selling book of the year.

分詞片語

由約翰所寫的書榮登年度最佳暢銷書。

在上述的例句中，我們用過去分詞片語 written by John 來形容前面的名詞（主詞）The book，表示這本書是由約翰所寫的（這本書被約翰所寫），而過去分詞 written 有被動的意思，如果將上述的例句改寫成複雜句中的形容詞子句，就不難了解為何過去分詞有被動的涵義了。

The book which was written by John is the best-selling

形容詞子句

book of the year.

由約翰所寫的書榮登年度最佳暢銷書。

在上述例句中，我們用限定形容詞子句 which was written by John 來形容前面的名詞（主詞）The book，而且用被動的型態 was written，而要將形容詞子句改寫成分詞片語的話，要先將關係代名詞 which 去掉，例句如下：

The book written by John is the best-selling book of the year.

如果把 which 去掉，整個句子出現二個動詞 was 和 is，而且混淆了主要子句和從屬子句的關係，因為 The book was written by John，在文法和意思上完全正確，而真正的主要子句 The book is the best-selling book of the year 反而被忽略了。在這種情況下，只能將形容詞子句中的 was 去掉，留下過去分詞 written，便成為被動的過去分詞片語後位修飾的典型句型。我們再將代表被動的過去分詞片語後位修飾的例句再練習一遍。

The young American voters <u>who were uninspired in 2008</u>
形容詞子句
presidential election would not vote for either Democrats or Republicans in the 2010 mid-term election.

The young American voters <u>uninspired in 2008 presidential</u>
分詞片語
election would not vote for either Democrats or Republicans in the 2010 mid-term election.

在 2008 年總統選舉不受鼓舞的美國年輕選民在 2010 年期中選舉時，也不會投票給民主黨員或共和黨員。

《經濟學人》這樣讀就對了

4-2 練習

▶ 請將下列句子中的後位修飾分詞片語找出來。

1. According to a poll conducted by The Pew Research Centre, 70% of the young voters, aged 18 to 30, tend to vote for the Democratic Party.

2. The earthquake drill, "Duck, Cover, and Hold" claimed to prepare Californians for "the big one", took place in Santa Monica's public schools yesterday.

3. Singapore Exchange Limited (SGX), Singapore's main stock exchange, is bidding for Australian Securities Exchange (ASX), and the merge will save the both bourses A$8.4 billion ($8.3 billion) reckoned by Morgan Stanley, an investment bank.

4. Todd Combs running a hedge fund in Connecticut is appointed by Warren Buffet, the chairman and chief executive of Berkshire Hathaway, a conglomerate holding company, as an investment manager.

5. Russia's President Dmitry Medvedev is scheduled to attend a NATO summit and signs a cooperation deal which is intend to repair relations damaged by NATO expansion in Eastern Europe.

6. The 2008 Mumbai terrorist attacks showed that jihadists based in Pakistan were able to launch bloody attack in India even though they were forced to camp in border regions.

7. HTC, a smartphone maker, is the first one to use Android operation system developed by Google. The bet pays off and HTC has taken a leading position in smartphone market.

8. The World Bank's report published by two scholars shows that any American goodwill gained from aid relief in the Central America has long term positive effect.

9. Thousands of Chinese student gathering at Beijing's Japan embassy asked the relief of seven fishing boat crew members arrested by the Japan Coast Guard on October 9th, 2010.

10. Metro-Goldwyn-Mayer (MGM), a Hollywood studio facing with $3 billion debt due in 2011, filed for Chapter 11 bankruptcy protection.

The studio was saddled with debt after a leveraged buyout (LBO) deal approved by the board.

📖 4-2 解答

1. *conducted by The Pew Research Centre*
   中譯：根據皮威研究中心所做的民意調查顯示，年齡介於 18 到 30 歲的年輕選民中，70% 要投給民主黨。

2. *claimed to prepare Californians for "the big one"*
   中譯：昨天聖塔摩尼卡的中小學進行地震演習「蹲下、尋求掩護和抓住掩護物」的演習，宣稱能幫助加州民眾準備將來的大地震。

3. *reckoned by Morgan Stanley, an investment bank*
   中譯：新加坡主要的證券交易所，新加坡證交所出價購併澳洲證券交易所，投資銀行摩根史坦利估計這項合併案將為二家證交所節省澳幣 84 億元（83億美元）支出。

4. *running a hedge fund in Connecticut*
   中譯：在康乃迪克州負責操盤避險基金的泰德·康柏斯被投資控股公司波克夏·哈薩威公司的董事長兼執行長華倫·巴菲特任命為投資長。

5. *damaged by NATO expansion in Eastern Europe*
   中譯：俄羅斯總統梅帝弟安排參加北大西洋公約組織高峰會，並且簽署一項合作協議，用以修補北大西洋公約組織在東歐不斷擴張所造成的傷害。

6. *based in Pakistan*
   中譯：2008 年孟買恐怖攻擊顯示就算被迫困守在邊界，基地在巴基斯坦的聖戰士仍然能夠在印度發動血腥的攻擊。

7. *developed by Google*
   中譯：智慧型手機製造商宏達電是第一個採用由 Google 所開發的 Android 作業系統，這項賭注押對了，宏達電已經在智慧型手機市場取得領先的位置。

8. *published by two scholars, gained from aid relief in the Central America*

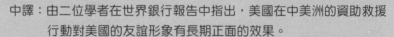

中譯：由二位學者在世界銀行報告中指出，美國在中美洲的資助救援
行動對美國的友誼形象有長期正面的效果。

9. *gathering at Beijing's Japan embassy, arrested by the Japan Coast
Guard on October 9th, 2010*

中譯：數千位的中國學生聚集在北京的日本大使館，要求釋放在 2010
年 10 月 9 日被日本海上防衛隊逮捕的 7 位漁船船員。

10. *facing with $3 billion debt due in 2011, approved by the board.*

中譯：面臨在 2011 年即將到期的 30 億美元負債，好萊塢的米高美
公司申請破產保護，米高美的負債來自由董事會核准的槓桿
融資購併案。

■4.3 分詞構句

在上一節中，我們將形容詞子句改寫成分詞片語，擺在名詞的後面，形成後位修飾的方式，來形容前面的名詞，但是在本節中我們將運用副詞子句改寫成分詞構句，擺在句首來形容主要子句的主詞，用以補充說明。

副詞子句是用來形容主要子句的形容詞、動詞或整個句子，表示時間順序、原因、條件或讓步的附帶狀況，例如：

When John has finished dinner, he goes out with Mary.

　　　　　副詞子句　　　　　　　　　　主要子句

當約翰用完晚餐後，他和瑪麗外出。

在副詞子句和主要子句中，主詞都是 John，而且副詞子句 has finished dinner 先發生，而後才和瑪麗外出。

因為副詞子句和主要子句的主詞都是同一個人 John，此時可以將副詞子句改寫成分詞構句，則整個句型變化就顯得比較活潑，例句如下：

Having finished dinner, John goes out with Mary.

　　　　分詞構句　　　　　　　　　主要子句

分詞構句依照主詞的主動和被動的意願，可以分成現在分詞構句和過去分詞構句。

★4-3-1 現在分詞構句

我們曾經說過分詞是由形容詞子句中的動詞加 ing 轉變而來，現在我們將副詞子句去掉副詞，而後將動詞加上 ing 保留受詞之後，便成為現在分詞構句，其句型結構如下：

副詞＋主詞＋動詞＋受詞，主詞＋動詞＋受詞

　　現在副詞子句　　　　　　　主要子句

動詞 ing＋受詞，主詞＋動詞＋受詞

　現在分詞構句　　　　主要子句

我們來看例句如下：

(1) After Vestas announced 3,000 job cuts, Vestas would close four factories in Denmark and Sweden.

(2) Announcing 3,000 job cuts, Vestas would close four factories in Denmark and Sweden.

威塔斯公司宣布裁員 3,000 名員工之後，將關閉在丹麥和瑞典的四座工廠。

在例句(1)中，我們用副詞子句 After Vestas announced 3,000 job cuts 來形容後面的名詞（主詞），但是整個句子還是屬於複雜句的結構，為了改變寫作技巧，增加句子的精簡性，所以用現在分詞構句擺在句首，來形容主詞 Vestas 形成例句(2)，有了分詞構句的加入，整個句子已經變得比較精采了，當然也顯示作者精湛的用字遣詞的技巧。

現在分詞構句在使用上顯示了句子中動詞（動作）的二種特性，分別是重疊性和接續性。重疊性表示主要子句和副詞子句中的動詞在時間上有重疊，說明這二個動詞有同時進行的意思，請看下面的例句：

(1) After Haitians drank contaminated water, Haitians see the wild spread of cholera which has killed more than 300 people.

(2) Drinking contaminated water, Haitians see the wild spread of cholera which has killed more than 300 people.

喝了受污染的飲用水後，海地民眾目睹大量擴散的霍亂病情，已造成超過 300 人的死亡。

在例句(2)中，現在分詞 drinking 和主要子句中的動詞 see 在時間上有重疊性，因為霍亂病情在海地民眾飲用了受污染的飲用水之後發生。

而持續性表示主要子句和副詞子句的動詞發生有先後順序，通常由副詞子句的完成式代表先發生的動作，而後再由主要子句的動詞接續發生，完全符合時態發生順序的文法原則；先發生者用完成式，後發生者用一般時態，我們來看下面的例句。

(1) After Haiti's Sacred Heart Hospital has treated more than 300 cholera patients in three days, the hospital is running out of medical supplies and calling for help.

(2) Having treated more than 300 cholera patients, Haiti's Sacred Heart Hospital is running out of medical supplies and calling for help.

　三天內治療了超過 300 位霍亂的病患後，海地的聖心醫院已經快用完醫療用品，呼籲外界給予援手。

　在上述的例句（1）中，副詞子句用現在完成式 After Haiti's Sacred Heart Hospital has treated more than 300 cholera patients in three days，代表先發生的事件，而後主詞才用完醫療用品並向外求援。

★4-3-2過去分詞構句

　本章第一節中曾說明過過去分詞有被動的意思，同樣的過去分詞構句也包含被動的意涵。

　過去分詞構句也就是將複雜句中被動的副詞子句，改寫成被動分詞構句，擺在句首來形容名詞，其句型結構如下：

<u>副詞＋主詞＋be動詞＋過去分詞＋受詞</u>，主詞＋動詞＋受詞
　　　　　　副詞子句　　　　　　　　　*主要子句*

<u>被動分詞＋受詞</u>，主詞＋動詞＋受詞
　被動分詞構句　　*主要子句*

我們來看下面的例句：

(1) When <u>Blythe Solar Power project was approved by</u>
　　　　　　　　　　　副詞子句

America's Department of the Interior, Blythe Solar Power project will be the world's largest solar energy project invested by a German Company.

(2) <u>Approved by America's Department of the Interior,</u> Blythe
　　　　　　　　　　過去分詞構句

Solar Power project will be the world's largest solar energy project invested by a German Company.

被美國內政部核准的拜斯太陽能發電計畫，將成為由德國廠商投資的全球最大太陽能計畫。

在例句(1)中，我們用被動的副詞子句 When Blythe Solar Power project was approved by America's Department of the Interior 來形容整個主要子句，這是典型的複雜句結構。而在例句(2)中，我們將副詞子句中的主詞 Blythe Solar Power project 和動詞 was 去掉，保留過去分詞 approved，而後形成過去分詞構句 Approved by America's Department of the Interior，擺在句首，來形容後面的句子 Blythe Solar Power project，形成過去分詞構句被動的句子結構。我們再看下面的例句：

(1) LimeWire was forced to cease operation after permanent court injunction. It is starting a new website to offer file-sharing service.

(2) Forced to cease operation after permanent court injunction, LimeWire is starting a new website to offer file-sharing service.

在法院永久性的禁止令強迫下，令埃（LimeWire）建立一個新的網站，提供檔案共享服務。

接下來我們來看一下，相同的單字，但是用現在分詞構句和過去分詞構句後所代表意義的不同。

(1) When David Cameron faces a record-breaking public debt, he decides to cut government spending by 20% and to increase personal income tax rate by 1%.

(2) Facing a record-breaking public debt, David Cameron decides to cut government spending by 20% and to increase personal income tax rate by 1%.

主動面對破紀錄的公債，大衛・卡麥隆決定要刪減 20% 的政府支出，同時增加個人綜合所得稅率 1%。

(3) Mikhail Khodorkovsky was faced with eight years prison sentence charge for tax evasion. He is prosecuted for another security fraud charge which is politically motivated.

(4) Faced with eight years prison sentence charge for tax evasion, Mikhail Khodorkovsky is prosecuted for another security fraud charge which is politically motivated.

被迫面對逃稅 8 年刑期指控，麥肯‧可丹科斯基又因違反證券交易法被起訴。一般視此項起訴背後有政治動機。

同樣都是 face（面對）這個單字，但是在例句(2)句中是現在分詞 facing，代表主詞 David Cameron 是主動面對破紀錄的公債問題。而在例句(4)句中是過去分詞 faced with，代表主詞 Mikhail Khodorkovsky 是被迫（被動）面對逃稅的 8 年刑期指控。從以上的分析不難看出，主詞在使用現在分詞構句（主動）和過去分詞構句（被動）的差別了。

4-3 練習

▶ 請將下列的副詞子句改寫成分詞構句，並且放在句首，形成完整的句子。

1. While Japan's defense budget has been cut each year, it is ranked in term of percent of GDP at the lowest among the Organization for Economic Cooperation and Development (OECD) countries.

2. After Google has been found by Britain's Information Ministry for beaching privacy protection law, it is reviewing its Mapping of Street service project.

3. After Dilma Rousseff won the Brazil's presidential election, she became Brazil's first female president.

4. While Dilma Rousseff urges the G20 countries to combat currency manipulation, Ms. Rousseff will hold a joint press conference at Seoul, South Korea, the host country of 2010 G20 summit.

5. After Sunni jihadists linked to al-Qaeda, they have launched several attacks in a town south of Baghdad and killed 110 Iraqi civilians.

6. After Sarah Palin has lead the Tea Party Movement in victory in mid-term election, she became the Republican favoured presidential candidate in 2012.

7. While America's economy was saddled with high unemployment and budget deficit, it grew by 2% in the second quarter at an annual rate.

8. After British Airways recovered from the second quarter losses, it reported its better than expected third quarter earings in term of £0.5 per share.

9. When Vodafone has decided to sell its minority steak of Softbank, Japan's second largest mobil phone operator, Vodafone is focusing its business on cloud computing sector.

10. When G20 leaders gather in Seoul, South Korea, on November 12th, 2010, they will discuess rising tenson of global fiscal deficit and currency wars caused by the U.S. and China.

📖4-3 解答

1. *Having been cut each year, Japan's defense budget is ranked in term of percent of GDP at the lowest among the Organization for Economic Cooperation and Development (OECD) countries.*
   中譯：每年被刪減的日本國防預算，按照國內生產毛額百分比來計算的話是經濟合作開發組織國家中最低的。

2. *Having been found by Britain's Information Ministry for beaching privacy protection law, Google is reviewing its Mapping of Street service project.*
   中譯：被英國資訊部發現違反私人隱私保護法後，Google 重新評估它的街景繪圖服務計畫。

3. *Winning the Brazil's presidential election, Dilma Rousseff became Brazil's female president.*
   中譯：贏得巴西總統大選後，笛瑪・羅賽夫成為巴西第一位女性總統。

4. *Urgeing the G20 countries to combat currency manipulation, Dilma Rousseff will hold a joint press conference at Seoul, South Korea, the host country of 2010 G20 summit.*
   中譯：督促 20 大工業國對抗外匯操控，笛瑪・羅賽夫將在 2010 年 20 大工業國高峰會主辦城市南韓首爾召開聯合記者會。

5. *Linking to al-Qaeda, Sunni jihadists have launched several attacks in a town south of Baghdad and killed 110 Iraqi civilians.*
   中譯：與蓋達有關的遜尼派聖戰士在巴格達南部小鎮發動數波攻擊，造成 110 位平民死亡。

6. *Having lead the Tea Party Movement in victory in mid-term election, Sarah Palin became the Republican favoured presidential candidate in 2012.*
   中譯：領導茶黨在期中選舉勝利的莎拉・培林，成為共和黨最受注目的 2012 年總統候選人。

7. *Saddled with high unemployment and budget deficit, America's economy grew by 2% in the second quarter at an annual rate.*

中譯：在高失業率和預算赤字拖累下，美國經濟在第二季以年率計算
的話成長 2%。

8. *Recovering from the second quarter losses, British Airways reported its better than expected third quarter earings in term of £0.5 per share.*

中譯：從第二季損失中反彈的英國航空公司發表高於預期的第三季獲
利盈餘，每股 0.5 英鎊。

9. *Having decided to sell its minority steak of Softbank, Japan's second largest mobil phone operator, Vodafone is focusing its business on cloud computing sector.*

中譯：決定出售日本第二大行動電話商軟體銀行的少數持股之後，維
達電信將其注意力擺在雲端運算上。

10. *Gathering in Seoul, South Korea, on November 12th, 2010, G20 leaders will discuess tenson of global fiscal deficit and currency wars caused by the U.S. and China.*

中譯：當 2010 年 11 月 12 日 20 大工業國領袖在南韓首爾聚會
時，他們將討論不斷增加的全球財政赤字和由美國與中國所
造成的貨幣戰爭。

第四章 綜合練習

▶ 請將下列文章中的形容詞子句改寫成分詞片語，副詞子句改寫成分詞構句。

Defense budgets which account at least 20% of annual government spending have been cut everywhere. Britian and France are cutting military spending by 6% over five years. After German has withdrawn its 5,000 armed force from Afghanistan, German is planning to cut its military spending by 10% for the next decade. Defense industries which are dominated by American and European companies are finding new tactic to protect their profits. Robert Gates, Defense Secretary of the United States, says that America will change its military contracts from "cost plus" to "fixed-price" method. Lockheed-Martin, which makes the F-35 jointed strike fighter jet, secures the $400 billion contract to produce 200 of them. While Boeing lobbies Saudi Arabia to buy 100 of its F-15, Boeing is asking Congress to approve its export sales to 30% of its defense business from 15%. Britain's BAE System and France's Dassault are aiming the replacement of NATO's aging nuclear submarines. Emerging economies, which include India, China and Brazil, are opening their wallets to purchase these sophisticated military equipments. Although defense budget has been cut, defense secretaries around the world always have big-ticket items on their shopping lists.

_____
_____
_____
_____
_____
_____

┃第四章 綜合練習解答┃

▶ 請將下列文章中的形容詞子句改寫成分詞片語，副詞子句改寫成分詞
構句（形容詞子句改寫成分詞片語，副詞子句改寫成分詞構句已用下
標線註明）。

Defense budgets accounting at least 20% of annual government spending have
been cut everywhere. Britian and France are cutting military spending by 6%
over five years. Having withdrawn its 5,000 armed force from Afghanistan,
German is planning to cut its military spending by 10% for the next decade.
Defense industries dominated by American and European companies are finding
new tactic to protect their profits. Robert Gates, Defense Secretary of the
United States, says that America will change its military contracts from "cost
plus" to "fixed-price" method. Lockheed-Martin making the F-35 jointed strike
fighter jet, secures the $400 billion contract to produce 200 of them. Lobbying
Saudi Arabia to buy 100 of its F-15, Boeing is asking Congress to approve its
export sales to 30% of its defense business from 15%. Britain's BAE System
and France's Dassault are aiming the replacement of NATO's aging nuclear
submarines. Emerging economies, including India, China and Brazil, are opening
their wallets to purchase these sophisticated military equipments. Although
defense budget has been cut, defense secretaries around the world always have
big-ticket items on their shopping lists.

第四章 單字

- ★memorial service 喪禮
- ★a fallen star 殞落的巨星
- ★a falling star 正在消失中的明星
- ★phenomenon 現象
- ★celebrity 名人
- ★tabloid magazine 八卦雜誌
- ★paparazzi 狗仔隊
- ★the Capitol Hill 國會山莊
- ★registered 已註冊的
- ★blocked 被封鎖的
- ★complain 抱怨信
- ★Twitter service 推特
- ★responsible for 負責
- ★Haze 霾害
- ★tribal people 原住民
- ★alarming levels 警戒水準
- ★peninsula 半島
- ★unrealiable 不可靠的
- ★statistics 統計數字
- ★unreported bonus 未申報紅利
- ★complicated property deals 複雜的土地交易
- ★unknown shady gifts 不可知的祕密禮物
- ★GDP per capital 每人國內生產毛額
- ★maths 數學
- ★engineering 工程
- ★computer science 電腦科技
- ★terrorists 恐怖分子
- ★photographs 相片
- ★London Heathrow Airport 倫敦希斯洛機場
- ★scan 掃描、檢查
- ★passangers 旅客
- ★terrorist attack 恐怖攻擊
- ★alarm 警報
- ★staff 員工
- ★computer software 電腦軟體
- ★participate 參與
- ★volunteer 志工
- ★Ho Chi Minh City, Vietnam 越南胡志明市
- ★the Peace Corp 和平志工團
- ★word of mouth 口碑
- ★proven 證明、有效的
- ★marketing strategy 行銷策略
- ★era 時代
- ★social networking 社群網
- ★stock market's free fall 股票市場重挫
- ★estimated 預估的
- ★retirement saving accounts 退休儲蓄帳戶
- ★401K 美國員工退休計畫
- ★suffer 遭受

★tremendous 重大的
★disqualified 無資格的
★homeowners 屋主
★Treasury Department 財政部
★mortgage 房地產貸款
★modification 修正
★under water 價值下跌
★woods 森林
★Whitney Houston 惠妮・休斯頓
★national anthem 國歌
★Super Bowl XXV 第 25 屆超級杯
★arrest 拘捕
★possession 持有
★marijuana 大麻
★uninspired 未受鼓舞的
★presidential election 總統選舉
★Democrats 民主黨員
★Republicans 共和黨員
★a poll 民調結果、民意調查
★conduct 實施、進行
★the Democratic Party
　美國民主黨
★drill 演習
★Duck, Cover, and Hold
　蹲下、尋求掩護和抓住掩護物
★claim 宣稱
★the big one 大地震
★stock exchange 證券交易所
★bid for 出價
★the merge 購併

★bourse 證交所
★Morgan Stanley 摩根史坦利
★an investment bank 投資銀行
★a hedge fund 避險基金
★appoint 指定
★Warren Buffet 華倫・巴菲特
★Chairman 董事長、主席
★Berkshire Hathaway
　波克夏・哈薩威公司
★conglomerate
　複合式、多角化投資
★holding company 控股公司
★schedule 安排、排程
★attend 參加
★cooperation deal 合作協議
★Mumbai 印度孟買
★Jihadists 聖戰士
★bloody 血腥的
★camp 基地、困守
★border 邊界
★operating system 作業系統
★pays off 押對寶了
★scholars 學者
★goodwill 友誼
★gain 獲得
★aid relief 救援行動
★the Central America 中美洲
★long term 長期的
★positive 正面的
★thousands 數以千計的

★Beijing 北京

★embassy 大使館

★relief 釋放

★fishing boat 漁船

★crew member 船員

★arrest 逮捕

★the Japan Coast Guard
日本海上防衛隊

★Metro-Goldwyn-Mayer（MGM）
米高美公司

★Hollywood 好萊塢

★studio 影城

★debt 負債

★file 申請

★bankruptcy 破產

★protection 保護

★saddle 加上

★leveraged buyout（LBO）
槓桿融資購併

★the board 董事會

★announce 宣布

★factory 工廠

★Denmark 丹麥

★Sweden 瑞典

★Haitians 海地民眾

★contaminated water
受污染的飲用水

★spread 散布

★cholera 霍亂

★sacred heart 聖心

★medical supplies 醫療用品

★approved 核准

★Department of the Interior
內政部

★solar energy 太陽能

★solar power 太陽能發電

★cease 停止

★permanent 永久的

★court injunction 法院禁止令

★file-sharing service
檔案共享服務

★record-breaking 破紀錄的

★public debt 公債

★government spending 政府支出

★personal income tax rate
個人綜合所得稅率

★tax evasion 逃稅

★prosecute 起訴

★security fraud 違反證券交易法

★politically 政治上的

★motivate 動機

★defense budget 國防預算

★rank 排名

★in term of 依此排名

★the Organization for Economic
Cooperation and Development
（OECD）經濟合作和開發組織

★ministry 部門

★breach 違反

★privacy protection laws
　個人隱私保護法

★review 評估

★presidential election 總統選舉

★female 女性

★president-elect 總統當選人

★Dilma Rouseff 笛瑪‧羅賽夫

★urge 督促

★combat 對抗

★currency manipulation 操控外匯

★a joint press conference
　聯合記者會

★the host country 主辦國

★al-Qaeda 蓋達（恐怖組織）

★Sunni jihadists 遜尼派聖戰士

★attack 攻擊

★Baghdad 巴格達

★Iraqi 伊拉克

★civilian 平民百姓

★Sarah Palin 沙拉‧培林

★victory 勝利

★favoured 滿意的、屬意的

★candidate 候選人

★budget deficit 預算赤字

★at an annual rate 年率計算

★the second quarter 第二季

★British Airways 英國航空公司

★recover 恢復、反彈

★losses 損失

★better than expected 高於預期

★minority steak 少數股權

★Vodafone 維達電信

★cloud computing 雲端運算

★defense budgets 國防預算

★account 占了多少（比率）

★military spending 軍事預算

★decade 10年

★dominate 占據

★tactic 方法、策略

★defense secretary 國防部長

★contract 合約

★cost plus 成本加成

★fixed-price 固定價格

★Lockheed-Martin
　洛克希德‧馬丁

★secure 取得、確保

★Boeing 波音公司

★Saudi Arabia 沙烏地阿拉伯

★lobby 遊說

★Congress 國會議員

★approve 核准

★BAE System 英國航太系統公司

★Dassault 達梭公司

★aim 對準

★replacement 替換

★nuclear submarines 核子潛艇

★sophisticated 精密的

★big-ticket items
　金額龐大的項目

第五章 動名詞和動名詞片語

在第四章中,我們將動詞字尾加上 ing 成為現在分詞或過去分詞的方式,轉型為形容詞擺在名詞的前面來形容後面的名詞,一個字的分詞擺在名詞的前面,而二個字以上的分詞片語則擺在名詞後面形成後位修飾,以上是動詞的另一種用法。在本章中,將介紹動詞的另一種用法:動名詞。

■5.1 動名詞

動名詞就是將動詞字尾加上 ing，成為動名詞，形成另一種型式的名詞，可作為句子中的主詞或受詞。動名詞和分詞最大的不同在於動名詞只有現在分詞的型態（Ving），沒有過去分詞的型態，而分詞則有現在分詞代表主動或進行中的狀態，過去分詞代表被動或已完成的狀態。動名詞的用法，例句如下：

Seeing is believing.

　　主詞 動詞　 受詞

眼見為憑。

在上述的例句中，我們用二個動名詞，分別是 Seeing 和 believing（原型是 see 和 believe）作為句子中的主詞 seeing 和受詞 believing，形成完整的句子。如果沒有將 see 和 believe 變成動名詞的話，會形成什麼樣的錯誤呢？我們來看一下例句：

See is believe. ……(×)

主詞 動詞 受詞

在上述的例句中出現三個動詞 see, is 和 believe，這違反了句子結構的嚴重錯誤——一個句子只能有一個動詞，為了避免此種錯誤，在此情況下，只能將 see 和 believe 分別加上 ing 變成動名詞，成為句子的主詞和受詞，形成合乎文法規定的完整句子結構。

接下來我們來看動名詞當主詞的用法，例句如下：

Smoking is not good for you.

　主詞　　　動詞　　　受詞

吸菸對你不好。

在上述的例句中，用動名詞 Smoking（原型動詞為 smoke）來代表句子的主句，如果用 smoke 來代表主詞的話，則又犯了句子中有二個動詞的錯誤。接下來看動名詞當受詞的例句：

We enjoy reading.

主詞 動詞　 受詞

我們喜歡閱讀。

在上述的例句中，我們用動名詞 reading（原型動詞為 read）來代表句子中的受詞，形成完整的句子結構。

5-1 練習

▶ 請將下列句子中的動名詞找出來。。

1. When President Obama visited India this week, President Obama stated that getting closer to Indian tiger would promote international trade between two countries.

2. Although Japan and the United States have different consideration of relocation of American Marine base in Okinawa, supporting the Asia security is still the major concern.

3. Liu Xiaobo, Chinese jailed activist, was barred from attending the Nobel Peace Prize award ceremony on December 10th held in Oslo, Norway.

4. California's Proposition 19, which legalizes the recreational use of marijuana, was repeatedly failing to pass the initative.

5. New York City, which is the pioneer of green projects, has taken several steps toward meeting its green goals.

6. When Cuba's politicians want to change the country's economic direction, they are just calling a congress of the ruling communist party, which is chaired by Raul Castro, Fidel Castro's young brother.

7. Repairing, building and plumbing are allowed at Cuba's economic reform bills.

8. Interpreting these economic changes is like reading tea leaves in a cup.

9. Boosting job creation is the major issue when Brazil's presiden-elect Dilma Rousseff takes office in January, 2011.

10. Giving is better than receiving.

5-1 解答

1. *getting*
   中譯：當歐巴馬總統本週訪問印度時，表示和印度保持密切關係有助提升二國之間的國際貿易。

2. *supporting*
   中譯：雖然日本和美國對於美國海軍陸戰隊在沖繩基地的遷移有不同考量，支持亞洲安全仍然是主要的考量。

3. *attending*
   中譯：被監禁的中國人士劉曉波被禁止參加 12 月 10 日在挪威奧斯陸舉行的諾貝爾和平獎頒獎典禮。

4. *failing*
   中譯：允許個人在休閒理由下合法使用大麻的加州公投案第 19 案，沒有通過公投的過關門檻。

5. *meeting*
   中譯：推動綠能減碳計畫先鋒的紐約市，已經採取許多方案來達成其既定的綠色目標。

6. *calling*
   中譯：當古巴政治人物需要改變古巴的經濟政策時，他們就要求由菲德·卡斯楚弟弟勞烏·卡斯楚所主導的共產黨召開會議。

7. *repairing, building, plumbing*
   中譯：維修、營建和水電維修是古巴經改法案中被允許的行業。

8. *interpreting, reading*
   中譯：解讀這些經濟改革就像在茶杯中看著茶葉說故事一般。

9. *boosting*
   中譯：增加就業機會是巴西總統當選人笛瑪·羅賽夫在 2011 年 1 月就任時的主要議題。

10. *giving, receiving*
    中譯：施比受更有福。

■5.2 動名詞片語

　　動名詞片語顧名思義就是以動名詞為開始，後面再加一個或二個以上的單字成為片語的結構，成為標準的動名詞片語，動名詞片語就是名詞，可以當句子中的主詞或受詞。當動名詞片語作主詞時應該視為單數，後面接單數動詞，我們來看下列動名詞片語當主詞的句子：

Working with non-governmental organizations (NGOs) in

　　　　　　　　　主詞（動名詞片語）

Haiti was a great experience for Bill Gates, a philanthropist.

　動詞　　　　　　　　　　受詞

和非政府組織在海地工作給慈善家比爾‧蓋茲很大的工作體驗。

　　在上述句子中，我們用動名詞片語 working with non-governmental organizations (NGOs) in Haiti 當作主詞，雖然 organizations 是一個複數名詞，但是重點還是在動名詞 working 身上，所以整個句子的動詞還是用單數動詞 was。接下來，我們來看動名詞片語當受詞的例子，例句如下：

Although American law schools are famous for their reputation, their counterparts in England and Germany are helping graduates to find jobs.

　受詞（動名詞片語）

雖然美國許多法學院以校譽著名，他們在英國和德國的競爭對手卻幫助畢業生找到工作。

　　在上述的例句中，用動名詞片語 helping graduates to find jobs 當作主要子句的受詞。

5-2 練習

▶ 找出下列句子中的動名詞片語。

1. Ermenegildo Zegna, a leading men's luxury clothing and leather goods firm in Italy, is working toward generational change.

2. In the 1980, Mr. Zegna started selling off-the-peg clothes and expanding product lines ranging from clothes to leather accessories.

3. Soaring tuition fees and increasing living expenses are preventing poor students from going to colleges.

4. When social networks like Facebook or Twitter are gaining adverting money, collecting consumer data on the net becomes very expensive.

5. Securing tax increase and spending cut were the major achievement of Portugal's opposition party.

6. Making music videos and consuming alcohol are cracked down by Iranian police.

7. Selling state property to business elite helps Burma's military junta to hold power.

8. Putting more private entrepreneurs at the sectors like retailing and manufacturing is the strategy China and Vietnam used in the 1990s.

9. Paying more attention to the poor's needs and taking responsibility of caregiving are the main goals of the Obama administration.

10. Satisfying customer's needs and guaranteeing money back are the key factors of Walmart's success.

5-2 解答

1. *working toward generational change*
   中譯：義大利著名的奢華男仕服裝和皮件商熱甘那，正朝著世代交替的步伐前進。

2. *selling off-the-peg clothes, expanding product lines*
   中譯：在 1980 年代熱甘那先生開始銷售成衣和擴充產品線從服裝到皮件相關製品。

3. *Soaring tuition fees, increasing living expenses, going to colleges*
   中譯：上漲的學雜費和生活費造成貧窮的學生無法上大學念書。

4. *gaining adverting money, collecting consumer data on the net*
   中譯：當臉書和推特等社群網逐漸吸引廣告資金時，在網路上蒐集消費者資料變成很昂貴。

5. *Securing tax increase and spending cut*
   中譯：確保增稅和刪減支出，是葡萄牙反對黨的主要成就。

6. *Making music videos, consuming alcohol*
   中譯：製作音樂錄影帶和喝酒等活動，被伊朗警方取締和禁止。

7. *Selling state property to business elite*
   中譯：將政府土地出售給紅頂商人，幫助緬甸軍政府掌握政權。

8. *Putting more private entrepreneurs at the sectors*
   中譯：鼓勵私人企業從事零售業和製造業是中國和越南在 1990 年代所採用的策略。

9. *Paying more attention to the poor's needs, taking responsibility of caregiving*
   中譯：重視窮人的需求和負起照顧弱勢是歐巴馬政府的二大目標。

10. *Satisfying customer's needs, guaranteeing money back*
   中譯：滿足顧客需求和不滿意保證退錢是威瑪量販店成功的關鍵因素。

第五章 綜合練習

▶ 請將下列文章中的動名詞和動名詞片語找出來。

Sorting out America's political and fiscal mess is not a difficult task. The only thing you need in the Capitol Hill is political courage. Political gridlock is expected. Asking spending cut is not welcomed. But President Obama can take the lead of domestic policy.

America's fiscal deficit is running at 9% of gross domestic production (GDP), the highest in the past 50 years. Increasing public spending and tax cutting for the last decade were to be blamed. Plugging this hole is easy if the economy is starting to recover and these stimulus plans are expired. America's tax system is like a Swiss cheese. There are holes everywhere, including exemptions, deductions and investment credits. Scrapping these distortions is not a difficult job. Flat tax rate system which was proposed by John McCain, a Republican senator from Arizona, is endorsed by both parties.

Drawing a plan to reduce the deficit to the manageable level is easy. Getting politicians to work together is another matter. Political gridlock is good for Republicans who are afraid of losing president nomination to a tea-party candidate if they bend on tax reform. Visiting Asian countries and attending G20 summit are the job President Obama likes. Paying attention to domestic issues is the president need to do now.

_____

_____

_____

_____

_____

_____

┃ 第五章 綜合練習解答 ┃

▶ 請將下列文章中的動名詞和動名詞片語找出來（動名詞和動名詞片語
已用下標線註明）。

Sorting out America's political and fiscal mess is not a difficult task. The only thing you need in the Capitol Hill is political courage. Political gridlock is expected. Asking spending cut is not welcomed. But President Obama can take the lead of domestic policy.

America's fiscal deficit is running at 9% of gross domestic production (GDP), the highest in the past 50 years. Increasing public spending and tax cutting for the last decade were to be blamed. Plugging this hole is easy if the economy is starting to recover and these stimulus plans are expired. America's tax system is like a Swiss cheese. There are holes everywhere, including exemptions, deductions and investment credits. Scrapping these distortions is not a difficult job. Flat tax rate system which was proposed by John McCain, a Republican senator from Arizona, is endorsed by both parties.

Drawing a plan to reduce the deficit to the manageable level is easy. Getting politicians to work together is another matter. Political gridlock is good for Republicans who are afraid of losing president nomination to a tea-party candidate if they bend on tax reform. Visiting Asian countries and attending G20 summit are the job President Obama likes. Paying attention to domestic issues is the president need to do now.

第五章 單 字

- ★India tiger
  印度老虎
  （代表印度是亞洲新興國家）
- ★promote 提升
- ★international trade 國際貿易
- ★consideration 考量
- ★relocation 遷移
- ★Marine 海軍陸戰隊
- ★Okinawa 沖繩
- ★concern 考慮
- ★jailed activist
  被監禁的異議人士
- ★bar 禁止
- ★attend 參加
- ★Oslo, Norway 挪威奧斯陸
- ★Proposition 19 公投案第19案
- ★legalize 合法
- ★recreational 休閒的
- ★initative 公投案
- ★pioneer 先鋒
- ★green projects 節能減碳計畫
- ★toward 朝向
- ★meet 達成
- ★Communist Party 共產黨
- ★Raul Castro 勞烏‧卡斯楚
- ★Fidel Castro 菲德‧卡斯楚
- ★reform 改革
- ★repair 修理
- ★build 建築

- ★plumb 水電維修
- ★allow 允許
- ★interprete 解讀、翻譯
- ★job creation 增加就業機會
- ★issue 議題
- ★president-elect 總統當選人
- ★non-governmental organizations (NGOs) 非政府組織
- ★a philanthropist 慈善家
- ★law schools 法學院
- ★reputation 校譽、商譽
- ★counterparts 競爭對手
- ★graduates 畢業生
- ★luxury clothing 奢華服裝
- ★leather goods 皮件
- ★toward 朝著
- ★generational change 世代交替
- ★off-the-peg clothes 成衣
- ★product lines 產品線
- ★ranging 範圍
- ★accessories 相關製品
- ★soar 增加
- ★tuition 學費
- ★fee 費用
- ★prevent 禁止、阻止
- ★Facebook 臉書
- ★Twitter 推特
- ★advertising 廣告

★expensive 昂貴的

★secure 確保

★tax increase 增稅

★spending cut 刪減費用

★achievement 成就

★Portugal 葡萄牙的

★opposition party 反對黨

★crack down 鎮壓、禁止、取締

★business elite 紅頂商人

★Burma 緬甸

★junta 軍政府

★entrepreneurs 企業

★sector 產業項目

★retailing 零售業

★manufacturing 製造業

★pay attention 重視、注意

★the poor 窮人

★needs 需求

★caregiving 照護

★the Obama administration 歐巴馬政府

★satisfy 滿足

★guarantee 保證

★key factors 關鍵因素

★sort out 找出

★mess 混亂問題

★task 工作

★the Capitol Hill 美國國會

★gridlock 僵持

★domestic policy 國內政策

★fiscal deficit 財政赤字

★gross domestic production (GDP) 國內生產毛額

★blame 責怪

★plug 堵住、修理

★recover 復甦

★including 包括

★cheese 起司

★exemption 免除、排除

★deduction 扣抵

★investment credit 投資抵免

★scrape 取消

★distortion 干擾、不正常

★endorse 簽署、保證

★nomination 提名

★candidate 候選人

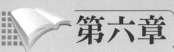

第六章　直接引用句和間接引用句

在《經濟學人》或一般英文週刊中，常引用事件當事人親口說的一句話或是當事人的看法，來表達新聞事件的真實性，這時候就必須回到英文寫作的二種基本句型：直接引用句和間接引用句。

■6.1 直接引用句

　　直接引用句代表這句話是由新聞事件當事人親口說出的一句話，而記者將這句話原封不動的節錄下來，放在文章中，強調新聞事件當事人的看法或意見。直接引用句的句型結構如下：

「主詞＋動詞＋受詞,」主詞＋say

或

「主詞＋動詞＋受詞,」says＋主詞

　　直接引用句的句型重點在於用引號 " " 來區分句子中直接引用句的句子結構，同時引用句中的動詞時態和主要子句的動詞時態不需要一致，因為引用句已經用引號 " " 將時態隔離了。我們來看下面的例句：

"In the United States you are always dating the company, " says John May.

約翰・梅爾說：「在美國你是和公司在約會」。

　　在上述的例句中，主詞約翰・梅爾（John May）親口說出 "In the United States you are always dating the company" 這句話，表達他對美國員工和僱主之間的勞資關係看法。值得注意的是，在直接引用句中的主詞 you 並不是代表一般英文中的「你」，而是泛指一般的普羅大眾。再看下面的例句：

Kiichiro Toyota's message is stark: "Corporate culture is killing Japan."

豐田章一郎的意圖赤裸裸的顯示「日本企業文化正在屠殺日本。」

　　在上述的例句中，豐田章一郎（豐田汽車的總裁）面對日本企業老人充斥，按年資升官的文化直接說出 "Corporate culture is killing Japan" 這句話，而在主要子句中則用冒號來引出這句直接敘述句。

　　有時記者並沒有直接引用說話者的完整句子，而只是針對句子中的一、二個單字來加以引用，以強調說話者的心情感受或意圖，我們來看下面的例句：

When teenagers cannot read or have trouble with numbers, Marie Hanson, a single mother, says it makes them "angry inside."

當年輕人有閱讀上的困難或對數字（數學）不太行時，單親母親瑪莉亞·漢斯說這些事讓年輕人「內心在生氣」。

在上述的例句中，主要子句中的主詞 Marie Hanson 針對年輕人在閱讀或數學有學習障礙時說出這些事讓年輕人"angry inside"這二個字，其實 Marie Hanson 在接受訪問時，說出一連串的話，記者在文章寫作中只畫龍點睛的引用這二個單字 "angry inside" 來點出問題的嚴重性。

而在《新聞週刊》(Newsweek)或其他雜誌中，為了增加雜誌的趣味性，都會專門開闢本週一句的專欄，附加說這句話的說話身分和說出這句話的背景說明，來博君一笑，我們來看下面的例句：

"Can't this country get a break?" U.N. spokesperson Imogen Wall says, after January's earthquake, July's flood and November's outbreak of cholera on Haiti.

海地經過一月的地震、七月的水災和十一月的霍亂疫情，聯合國發言人伊瑪根·沃爾說：「這個國家可不可以稍微休息一下？」。

在上述的例句中，聯合國發言人於海地在 2010 年歷經大地震、水災之後，在11月分又爆發霍亂疫情，面對多災多難的海地忍不住說出 "Can't this country get a break?" 這一句話，祈求上帝的憐憫。

在口語式的新聞報導中（例如電視或電臺）有時會用到直接引用句，引述當事人的說法，此時為了區分主播的報導內容和事件當事人的說法直接引用，所以用口語朗讀時必須有特殊的念法來加以區分直接引用句，我們來看下面的例句：

"Trading goes down, trading goes up." Jamie Dimon of JP Morgan Chase, an investment bank, told reporters in April.

摩根大通投資銀行的詹姆·迪謀在四月分告訴記者：「成交量有時下降，有時增加」。

在電視或新聞廣播中，要將這句念出來時，就必須將引號用 quote 念出來，讓收聽者明瞭這是一句直接引用句，其口語朗讀法如下：

Quote trading goes down, trading goes up, quote Jamie Dimon of JP Morgan Chase, an investment bank, told reporters in April.

我們在直接引用句的句首和句尾分別加念 quote，用以代表引號（" "）讓閱聽者在聽新聞廣播節目時，能明瞭這是直接引用句。

《經濟學人》這樣讀就對了

🖋 6-1 練習

▶ 請根據前後文的意思，將下列句子的直接引用句中的主詞找出來，並將全句翻譯成中文。

1. "You have to see it to believe," said Ms. Hanson. Ms. Hanson is running online maths tutoring.

2. "Because we know who you are, we can put good content to meet your needs," says Mark Euckerberg, the boss of Facebook, the world's biggest social network.

3. "He thinks that democracy stands in his way," says Mikhal Gorbachev, former Soviet leader. Mr. Gorbachev claims that Prime Minister Vladimir Putin is undermining Russia's democracy by clashing opposition voices.

4. Pascal Remy, a former chief editor of Michelin Guide, says "You win over the hearts of the Japanese and you sell tires." Michelin Guide was criticized the controversy surrounding of high number of three-star restaurants in Japan's Kansai region.

5. "What we promise we will deliver" was one of the short sentence sent by one of the G20 leaders after their summit in Seoul, South Korea.

6. "We want to keep domestic production. But we are quickly losing competitiveness," one of Toyota's executives said. Toyota has produced 60% of its vehicles abroad.

7. "This is a country where the mindset is all about input. They don't value output," says Heang Chhor, head of Mckinsey in Japan. Japan's workers are paid by seniority-based plan.

8. "Uncle Sam, you delivered…overall your actions were remarkably effective," says Warren Buffett, a billionaire. Mr. Buffett wrote an open letter to the U.S. government and thanked it for its bailout and stimulus plans.

9. Aung San Suu Kyi says "If we want to get what we want, we have to do it in the right way." Miss Suu Kyi, the Burmese opposition

leader, spoke to her supporters after being released after seven years of house arrest.

10. "Although many manufacturers have jumped ship to Bangladesh, Vietnam and Malaysia, most of America's imports is still "made in China", " says Tim Liaw, head of Nomura Securities, Hong Kong. Many foreign manufacturers are facing rising production cost in China.

6-1 解答

1. *you*（指讀者）

   漢斯小姐說：「你必須親眼看到才會相信（眼見為憑）」。漢斯小姐經營線上數學家教。

2. *We*（指*Facebook*）

   全球最大的社群網站臉書的老闆馬克・日博格說：「因為我們知道你是誰，因此我們能將好的內容放在網站來符合你的需求」。

3. *He*（指*Prime Minister Vladimir Putin*）

   前蘇聯領導人戈巴契夫說：「他認為民主擋住他的去路」。戈巴契夫宣稱總理浦亭透過壓迫反對聲音的方式，摧殘俄羅斯的民主。

4. *you*（指*Michelin*）

   米其林評鑑的前主編巴可・雷米說：「你贏得日本人的心，然後賣輪胎給他們」，米其林評鑑被批評在日本關西地區給予眾多的米其林三星級餐廳評等。

5. *We*（指 *G20 leaders*）

   在南韓首爾的 20 大工業國高峰會後，20 大工業國的領袖之一說：「我們承諾的，我們都會做到。」

6. *We*（指 *Toyota*）

   豐田汽車的一位主管說：「我們想要在國內生產，但是我們很快就失去競爭力。」豐田 60% 的汽車在海外生產。

7. *country*（指 *Japan*），*they*（指日本人）

   日本麥肯錫顧問公司主管漢銀・柯荷說：「這是一個只重視投入心態的國家，他們不重視產出」，日本員工按照年資高低敘薪。

8. *Uncle Sam*（指美國政府），*your actions*（指美國政府的紓困和振興計畫）

   億萬富翁華倫・巴菲特說：「美國政府所做的……政府所做的真是特別的有效。」巴菲特的公開信稱讚美國政府的紓困和刺激計畫。

9. *We*（指翁山蘇姬的支持者）

   翁山蘇姬說：「如果我們要得到我們想要的，就必須按照正確的方式去做」，緬甸反對黨領導人蘇姬在經過 7 年軟禁被釋放後對著她的支持者講話。

10. *many manufacturers*（指外國製造商）

野村證券香港總裁提姆‧廖說：「雖然許多製造商已經轉移到孟加拉、越南和馬來西亞生產，大部分的美國進口商品還是『中國製造』」，許多外國生產商面臨中國不斷上升的生產成本。

■6.2 間接引用句

間接引用句代表記者在寫作時，將新聞當事人所要表達的意見寫出來，但是透過記者的筆寫出來，其效果當然比不上直接引用句來的強烈，間接引用句的句型結構如下：

主詞＋says(said)＋that＋主詞＋動詞＋受詞

主要子句　　　　　　名詞子句

間接引用句的句型基本上，就是第二章我們所介紹的複雜句的結構，我們來看下面的例句：

The United Nations' Food and Agriculture Organization said

主詞　　　　　　　　　　　　　　　　動詞

that cost of world's food imports may exceed $1 trillion in 2010.

名詞子句

聯合國農糧署說全世界進口糧食的成本，在 2010 年時將超過 1 兆美元。

在上述的例句中，主要子句的主詞是 The United Nations' Food and Agriculture Organization，動詞 said，而受詞就是後續的 that 名詞子句 that cost of world's food imports may exceed $1 trillion in 2010。整句話就是聯合國農糧署根據相關資料說明 2010 年全球進口食品價格上漲的事實。有時在間接引用句中連接詞 that 可以省略，我們來看下面的例句：

Venezuela's president, Hugo Chavez, said he would

主詞　　　　　　　　　　　　　　　動詞

promote General Henry Rangel to be the army's commander-in-

名詞子句

chief.

委內瑞拉總統查維茲說他將提拔哈利·雷給將軍為陸軍總司令。

在上述的例句中，主要子句的主詞為 Venezuela's president, Hugo Chavez，動詞為 said，而後跟著名詞子句 he would promote General Henry Rangel to be the army's commander-in-chief.

而在間接引用句的主要子句常用的動詞 say（said）之外為 reckon（猜想、認為），我們來看下面的例句：

President Obama did not reckon that the underlying

<u>主詞</u>   <u>動詞</u>

problems in our current system were high unemployment and

<u>名詞子句</u>

huge budget deficit.

歐巴馬總統不認為目前美國的問題在於高失業率和大量的預算赤字。

在上述的例句中，我們在主要子句中用動詞 reckon 代替 said，來帶出整個受詞（名詞子句）that the underlying problems in our current system were high unemployment and huge budget deficit.

有時記者對於不太能確定新聞事件的正確性，或在截稿時間壓力下無法馬上查證的條件下，只好用 be reported（報導）的被動句型結構，我們來看例句：

Kim Jong-il, the great leader of Democratic People's Republic of Korea, is reported to undergo brain surgey after suffering a minor stroke.

朝鮮民主人民共和國領袖金正日據報導在中風之後進行腦部手術。

在上述的例句中，金正日中風的謠言四起，作者無法確認這事件的真實性，再加上北韓對於新聞的封鎖無法查證，只好用據報導 is reported 來報導整件事件。

有時寫作記者會以「不記名的消息來源」的字眼，來表示其新聞報導的正確性，我們來看下面的例句：

According to unanimous source, the United States was launching several cyber attacks against Iran's nuclear program by spreading Stuxnet, a sophisticated new type of malicious software.

根據不具名的消息來源指出，美國透過散播新型精密的 Stuxnet 惡意攻擊程式，對伊朗的核子計畫展開數次的網路攻擊。

在上述的句子中，記者用介系詞片語 according to unanimous source（不記名的消息來源）來帶出整個句子。

6-2 練習

▶ 請將下列句子中的間接引用句找出來。

1. Tim Clinton of EMI, a British struggling music company, said that the firm had reached an agreement with Apple's iTunes to download Beatles' albums.

2. Bob Steel, New York's deputy mayor, says the City's economy strength is stronger than many think, with education and health care industries doing well.

3. Facing increasing inflation, emerging market leaders are reported to consider fiscal no-nos like capital controls and currency intervention.

4. Ireland, says the country's finance minister, Brian Lenihan, doesn't need a bailout either from the IMF or the European Union.

5. Yoplait, a French yogurt firm, is said to be brought by General Mills, an American food firm. Danone, the world's biggest maker of yogurt, is running neck-and-neck with Yoplait in America.

6. Angela Merkel, Chancellor of Germany, said if borrowers were unable to repay their debts, their creditors were ought to bear the losses.

7. Microleading, says Sam Daley, director of the Microcredit Summit Campaign, is under attack and goes through a near-death experience.

8. Eugene Fama, a professor of the University of Chicago Booth School of Business, says that in the long term share prices tend to perform "random walk" which supports his efficient market hypothesis.

9. Angela Marinoni says although the Himalayas and Tibetan plateau are referred to as the Earth's third pole, the area is under an onslaught of air pollution.

10. Although the emergency reliefs and medical supplies have arrived in Haiti, doctors say that cholera has not peak and is likely to last months if water-chlorination facilities are not ready immediately.

6-2 解答

1. *the firm had reached an agreement with Apple's iTunes to download Beatles' albums*
   中譯：陷入困境的英國音樂公司科藝百代的提姆‧克林頓說，該公司已和蘋果公司的 iTunes 達成協議，可以下載披頭四的專輯。

2. *the City's economy strength is stronger than many think, with education and health care industries doing well*
   中譯：紐約市副市長鮑伯‧史提爾說，紐約市的經濟遠比其他人想像的好，尤其是教育和保健產業。

3. *to consider fiscal no-nos like capital controls and currency intervention*
   中譯：面對上升的通貨膨脹壓力，據報導開發中國家的領導人考慮採取許多不該做的措施，像是資本管制和外匯干預。

4. *Ireland doesn't need a bailout either from the IMF or the European Union*
   中譯：愛爾蘭的財政部長布萊恩‧李漢說，愛爾蘭不需要來自國際貨幣基金會或歐盟的紓困。

5. *to be brought by General Mills, an American food firm*
   中譯：法國優格製造商優沛蕾據說要被美國食品廠通用食品所收購。全球最大優格製造商戴那和優沛蕾在美國市場競爭激烈。

6. *if borrowers were unable to repay their debts, their creditors were ought to bear the losses*
   中譯：德國總理梅克爾說如果借款人無能力償還其負債的話，債權人也應該承擔放款的損失。

7. *Microleading is under attack and goes through a near-death experience*
   中譯：微型貸款高峰會主任山姆‧達利說微型貸款正在遭受攻擊，並且經歷近乎死亡的過程。

8. *that in the long term share prices tend to perform "random walk" which supports his efficient market hypothesis*

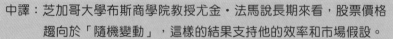

中譯：芝加哥大學布斯商學院教授尤金‧法馬說長期來看，股票價格
　　　趨向於「隨機變動」，這樣的結果支持他的效率和市場假設。

9. *although the Himalayas and Tibetan plateau are referred to as the Earth's third pole, the area is under an onslaught of air pollution*

中譯：安潔利亞‧馬利那亞說雖然喜馬拉雅山脈和西藏高原被稱之為
　　　地球的第三極，該地區正遭受空氣污染。

10. *that cholera has not peak and is likely to last months if water-chlorination facilities are not ready immediately*

中譯：雖然緊急救援和醫療用品已經到達海地，醫生說如果水加氯
　　　殺菌處理設施沒有馬上設置的話，霍亂的疫情還沒達到高
　　　峰，還有可能會持續數月之久。

第六章 綜合練習

▶ 請將下列文章中的直接引用句和間接引用句找出來。

"Color revolutions are everywhere in the world," says William Schreiber, an associate professor of Boren National Security. On December 2nd, 2010, people of Moldova, the poorest country in the Europe, will go to the polls for the parliamentary election. Hillary Clinton, State Secretary of the United States, says "This is the chance that democracy can root in the former Eastern Bloc of communists." In April 2009, young protesters stormed Moldova's Parliament building and chanted anti-communist slogans when the results of rigged election were announced. Dana Fort, a 25 years old jobless youth, says young Moldovan want to have European living standard. That is beyond everyone touch when the communist won last April election.

Countries without democracy can never joint the European Union. Experts said that the West should help the young Moldovan to accommodate their thirst for change. Damon Wilson of Atlantic Council, a think tank, says "That isn't 1989 in Moldova." "When you have the opportunity to govern a country like Moldova, you need to delivery what you have promised," he says. Ukraine, where Orange Revolution didn't bring stability to the country, is the lesson the West had learned the hard way. "Whoever wins the Sunday's election, that is a color revolution in Moldova, "says unanimous expert who observed 2009 election. The West should offer mentorship in state building for this young country. Moldovan, says President Obama, will lead the country to prosperity.

_____

_____

_____

_____

第六章 綜合練習解答

▶ 請將下列文章中的直接引用句和間接引用句找出來。（直接引用句和間接引用句已用下標線標示出來）

"Color revolutions are everywhere in the world," says William Schreiber, an associate professor of Boren National Security. On December 2nd, 2010 people of Moldova, the poorest country in the Europe, will go to the polls for the parliamentary election. Hillary Clinton, State Secretary of the United States, says "This is the chance that democracy can root in the former Eastern Bloc of communists." In April 2009, young protesters stormed Moldova's Parliament building and chanted anti-communist slogans when the results of rigged election were announced. Dana Fort, a 25 years old jobless youth, says young Moldovan want to have European living standard. That is beyond everyone touch when the communist won last April election.

Countries without democracy can never joint the European Union. Experts said that the West should help the young Moldovan to accommodate their thirst for change. Damon Wilson of Atlantic Council, a think tank, says "That isn't 1989 in Moldova." "When you have the opportunity to govern a country like Moldova, you need to delivery what you have promised," he says. Ukraine, where Orange Revolution didn't bring stability to the country, is the lesson the West had learned the hard way. "Whoever wins the Sunday's election, that is a color revolution in Moldova, " says unanimous expert who observed 2009 election. The West should offer mentorship in state building for this young country. Moldovan, says President Obama, will lead the country to prosperity.

第六章 單 字

- ★date 約會
- ★Kiichiro Toyota 豐田章一郎
- ★message 意圖、企圖
- ★stark 赤裸裸的
- ★teenager 年輕人
- ★tutor 家教
- ★content 內容
- ★get a break 休息一下
- ★spokesperson 發言人
- ★U. N. 聯合國
- ★Mikhal Gorbachev 戈巴契夫
- ★Vladimir Putin 浦亭
- ★Russia 俄羅斯
- ★clash 壓迫、迫害
- ★oppostion voices
  反對人士的聲音
- ★chief editor 主編
- ★Michelin Guide 米其林評鑑
- ★controversy 有爭議
- ★surrounding 周遭
- ★three-star restaurants
  三星級的餐廳
- ★Kansai region 關西地區
- ★promise 承諾
- ★deliver 做到、達成
- ★competitiveness 競爭力
- ★executive 主管
- ★vehicles 車輛
- ★abroad 海外

- ★mindset 心態
- ★value 珍惜
- ★Mckinsey 麥肯錫
- ★seniority-based 按年資計算
- ★Uncle Sam 美國（美國政府）
- ★remarkably 特別、傑出的
- ★an open letter 公開信
- ★bailout 紓困
- ★stimulus 刺激
- ★Aung Sam Suu Kyi 翁山蘇姬
- ★Burmese opposition leader
  緬甸反對黨領袖
- ★supporters 支持者
- ★release 釋放
- ★house arrest 軟禁
- ★manufacturer 製造商
- ★jump ship
  跳船（轉移生產基地）
- ★Bangladesh 孟加拉
- ★Vietnam 越南
- ★Malysia 馬來西亞
- ★imports 進口商品
- ★Nomura Securities 野村證券
- ★production cost 生產成本
- ★The United Nations' Food and
  Agriculture Organization
  聯合國農糧署組織
- ★trillion 兆
- ★promote 提拔

★army's commander-in-chief 陸軍總司令

★reckon 猜想、認為

★underlying problems 目前的問題

★huge 巨大的

★budget deficit 預算赤字

★Kim Jong-il 金正日

★undergo 遭受、接受、進行

★surgey 手術

★suffer 遭受

★stoke 中風

★unanimous 不具名的

★cyber attack 網路攻擊

★against 對抗

★sophisticated 精密

★malicious 惡意的

★EMI 科藝百代公司

★struggle 掙扎、陷入困境的

★agreement 協議

★download 下載

★deputy mayor 副市長

★economy strength 經濟強項

★consider 考慮

★fiscal 財政上的

★no-nos （許多）不該做的事

★capital control 資本管制

★currency intervention 外匯干預

★the IMF 國際貨幣基金會

★the European Union 歐盟

★Yoplait 優沛蕾

★yogurt 優格

★General Mills 通用食品

★Danone 戴那

★neck-and-neck 競爭激烈

★borrower 借款人

★unable 無能力的

★repay 償還

★ought 應該

★creditor 債權人

★bear 承擔

★losses 損失

★microleading 微型貸款

★attack 攻擊

★near-death 近乎死亡

★Eugene Fama 尤金・法馬

★long term 長期

★share price 股票價格

★tend 趨向於

★perform 表現

★random walk 隨機漫步

★support 支持

★efficient-market hypothesis 效率市場假設

★the Himalayas 喜馬拉雅山脈

★Tibetan plateau 西藏高原

★pole 極地

★onslaught 遭受屠殺

★air pollution 空氣污染

★emergency 緊急

★reliefs 救援

★medical supplies 醫療用品

★peak 尖峰、高點

★water-chlorination
水加氯殺菌處理

★facilities 設施

★revolutions 革命

★Moldova 摩爾多瓦

★the polls 投票所

★parliamentary 國會

★election 選舉

★Hillary Clinton
希拉蕊·柯林頓

★State Secretary 國務卿

★democracy 民主

★root 生根

★Eastern Bloc 東歐

★communist 共產黨

★protester 示威者

★storm 衝破、衝入

★Parliament building 國會大樓

★slogan 口號

★rigged election 被操控的選舉

★announce 宣布

★jobless 失業的

★accommodate 達成

★thirst 渴望

★Ukraine 烏克蘭

★the West 西方國家

★mentorship 指導

★prosperity 繁榮

第七章 數字的閱讀

導 論

　　在《經濟學人》的文章中運用到許多數字，例如百分比或增加減比率來補充說明新聞事件的內涵，同時突顯問題的嚴重性，因此在本章中將針對數字的閱讀做說明，分別是百分比數字、增加減比率和金額寫法。

■7.1 百分比數字

在百分比數字的句型結構中，通常都是用民意機構做主詞，然後用名詞子句帶出百分比，其結構如下：

主詞＋同位語＋動詞（shows／states／reports）＋that＋名詞（百分比）＋動詞＋受詞

名詞子句

我們來看下面的例句：

A poll conducted by Pew, a research firm, shows that
主詞　　　　　　　　　　　　　　　　　　　　　動詞
50 percent of foreign home buyers in the United States are
名詞子句
residents of Canada, Mexico, the United Kingdom and China.

根據民調公司 Pew 的調查顯示，在美國房地產的外國買家中，有 50% 來自加拿大、墨西哥、英國和中國。

在上述的例句中，我們用主詞 A poll 作為主要子句的主詞，同時用被動分詞和同位語的方式介紹這份調查是由民調公司 Pew 所主導的 conducted by，而後用動詞 shows 帶出整個名詞子句 that 50 percent of foreign home buyers in the United States are residents of Canada, Mexico, the United Kingdom and China。

接下來，我們來看用分數的英語句子寫法：

Two-thirds of Americans approve full-body X-Ray airport scanners according to CBS News Poll.

根據哥倫比亞廣播公司新聞民調的調查，三分之二的美國人同意機場使用全身的 X 光檢查方法。

在上述例句中，我們用三分之二的美國人 Two-thirds of Americans 作為主詞，而後用動詞 approve 來帶出後續的受詞 full-body X-Ray airport scanners according to CBS News Poll。在英語幾分之幾的寫法中，分子用一般的英文數字 one, two, three……，但是分母卻用序數數字 third, fourth, fifth…… 來表示，例如五分之一就是 one-fifth，此種寫法有利於文章朗讀時，閱聽人只要聽到此種念法就知道這是分數的數字，值得注意的是，只要分子大於1，則此分數就是複數，而且複數的 s 要加在分母，形成複數的分數，例如五分之三的英文寫法為 three-fifths，而複數的分數作為主詞時，則隨後之動詞也必須用複數動詞，例句如下：

According to a poll conducted by Gallup, a market research firm, three-fifths of Americans believe that the government's bailout plan is helping "Wall Street" not "Main Street".

根據民調公司蓋洛普所做的調查顯示，五分之三的美國民眾相信政府的紓困計畫只在幫助華爾街金融業，而不是一般的老百姓。

在上述的例句中，以介系詞片語 according to a poll conducted by Gallup, a market research firm 做開頭，而後帶出整個主要子句和後續的名詞子句。

接下來我們來看分數的另一種寫法（分子 out of 分母；two out of three），例句如下：

Google, a search engine, handles two out of three online search a day in America which accounts 2 billion searches a given day.

搜索引擎 Google 每天處理美國每日 20 億筆搜尋量作業的三分之二量。

在上述的例句中，用 two out of three 的方式來代表三分之二（2／3），這種寫法有異於傳統的三分之二（2／3）（two-thirds）的寫法，增加了文章閱讀的變化性。接下來我們來看英文序數的寫法：

Yukio Hotoyama, the fourth Japan's prime minister in a row to last less than a year and the fourteenth prime minister for the past 20 years, announced his resignation on June 3th, 2010.

Many PMs, including Taro Aso, Yasuo Fukuda, Shinzo Abe, and Yoshiro Mori, are the heirs of political dynasties without any leadership skills.

日本連續第四位上任不到一年而且是二十年來第 14 位首相的鳩山由紀夫首相在 2010 年 6 月 3 日宣布辭職，包括麻生太郎、福田康夫、安倍晉三和森喜郎一樣的許多日本首相，都是政治家族的後代，卻缺乏任何的領導技巧。

在上述的例句中，我們在同位語中用二個序數來形容主詞 Yukio Hotoyama，分別是 the fourth Japan's prime minister 和 the fourteenth prime minister for the past 20 years。透過這種序數的方式，可以清楚了解到句子中主詞在文章中的詳細背景說明。

7-1 練習

▶ 請將下列句子中的分數、百分比等數字找出來。

1. Haiti, a falling state, is in the search for help. More than 60 percent of the 10 million population are living below the poverty line, an income of less than $1 per day per head.

2. One recent study found that America college enrollment could fall by 4.0 percent due to 2008 credit crisis and housing bust.

3. According to a poll counducted by Pew, a research firm, three-fifths of foreign executives working in China think that China violates human rights by imposing internet censorship.

4. Although Global Climate Change Summit was held in a snow-capped mountain resort of Switzerland, three out of five delegents attending the summit though the rich countries should take responsibility of reducing carbon dioxide emission, the major cause of green house effect.

5. Google's growth in term of sales revenue slowed to 9% in 2009, which indicates the firm's glorous day may be over.

6. Although Google is facing Facebook's onslaught on internet ads, its fourth quarter sales revenue rose by 20% to $6 billion, which beat most analysts' expectations.

7. Android, a smartphone operating system developed by Google, accounts for 28 percent of the market, but its archrival, Apple's iPhone, still dominates the market with 35 percent market share.

8. People below 30 will account for two-thirds of all growth in consumer spending in China over the next decade.

9. 75% of Europeans think that easy money, budget deficit, high unemployment and unsustainable social welfare, are the major causes of financial miseries in the euro zone.

10. According to a report published by Gallup, a market research firm, three out of five people it surveyed found that the West will shift from carbon-based economies to alternative-energy-based economies in few years.

《經濟學人》這樣讀就對了

📖7-1 解答

1. *60 percent*

中譯：衰退中的國家海地正在尋求協助，海地全國 1,000 萬人口中有超過 60% 的人生活在一人一天不到一塊美元收入的貧窮線下。

2. *4.0 percent*

中譯：最近的一項研究顯示，因為 2008 年信用危機和房地產崩盤事件，美國大學入學率可能下降 4%。

3. *three-fifths*

中譯：根據民調公司 Pew 的民調顯示，三分之二在中國工作的外國主管認為，中國網路審查的方式違反基本人權。

4. *three out of five*

中譯：雖然全球氣候變遷高峰會在瑞士白雪覆蓋高山上的渡假村舉辦，五分之三的出席代表認為富有國家有責任降低造成溫室效應的二氧化碳排放量。

5. *9%*

中譯：Google 的成長以營業額來計算的話在 2009 年只有 9%，可能代表該公司輝煌的日子可能結束了。

6. *fourth quarter, 20%*

中譯：雖然 Google 面對 Facebook 在網路廣告的猛攻，它第四季的營業收入增加 20% 達到 20 億美元，打敗分析師的預估。

7. *28 percent, 35 percent*

中譯：由 Google 所開發的智慧型手機作業系統 Android 占有 28% 的市場，但是它的競爭對手蘋果 iPhone 仍然主宰整個市場，擁有 35% 的市場占有率。

8. *two-thirds*

中譯：中國未來 10 年消費成長的動能有三分之二來自 30 歲以下民眾的消費力。

9. *75%*

中譯：75% 的歐洲人認為多餘的資金、預算赤字、高失業和無法支撐

　　　　　的社會福利，是造成歐元區金融苦楚的主要原因。

10. *three out of five*

　　中譯：根據蓋洛普所出版的報告指出，它所調查的 5 個人中有 3 個人認為未來幾年內，西方國家將從以碳為基礎的經濟轉變為以替代能源為基礎的經濟。

■7.2 增加減比率

在《經濟學人》的文章中,最喜歡用不同年度的增加減比率,例如二個年度的營業額增加減比率,來突顯問題的嚴重性,此種最常用句型如下:

主詞+動詞+to ×× in 2010 from ×× in 2009.

我們來看下面的例句:

Fitch, a rating agency, downgraded General Motor's long-term debt to "BBB" which reflected its earnings decline to $20 billion in 2010 from $25 billion in 2009.

信用評等機構惠譽調降通用汽車的長期負債至「BBB」等級,反應了通用獲利盈餘從 2009 年的 250 億美元下降到 2010 年的 200 億美元。

在上述的例句中,我們用形容詞子句來反應通用汽車被調降評等的理由,因為在 2010 年和 2009 年之間獲利下降 its earings decline to $20 billion in 2010 from $25 billion in 2009。我們用 to-from 從新到舊來界定二個時間點,而且英文的寫作重視最新的發展,所以把新的發展擺在 to 的後面,而比較早期的發展放在 from 的後面,這點和中文的寫作翻譯有很大的不同(從舊到新),需特別注意,再來看下面的例句:

Ireland, the Celtic tiger which is used to compare with Asian tigers, had achieved export-led growth, and its annual economic growth averaged 7% from 1988 to 2000.

常被用來和亞洲小龍做比較的愛爾蘭之虎的愛爾蘭,達成由出口帶動的成長,在 1988 年和 2000 年之間平均每年經濟成長率達到 7%。

在上述的例句中,我們的時間點為 from 1988 to 2000 之間,而經濟成長率用平均每年 7% 來形容 annual economic growth averaged 7%,值得注意的是在《經濟學人》的許多數據都是以年化的數據 annualized 來做表示:

Although the Fed's Quantitative Easing 2.0 (QE2.0) may increase the risk of inflation, loose monetary policy may creat more jobs, more jobs mean more income and consumer spending. In September wages rose at an annual rate of 8%.

雖然聯邦儲備銀行的第 2 回量化寬鬆政策可能增加通貨膨脹的風險,寬鬆的貨幣政策或許能增加就業機會,就業的增加代表收入增加和消費增加，在九月時工資以 8% 的年化率增加。

在上述的例句中，九月分的工資已公告，但是為了求得每個月比較基礎的平等，所以用年化率 annual rate 來表示，這樣的話才可以和每個月的數據做比較。接下來我們來看用 compared with 所做不同期間內數字的比較。

Morgan Stanley's share is trading at 25% below its book value, compared with 30% above for Goldman Sachs.

和高盛的股價交易價格高於其帳面值 30% 比較起來，摩根史坦利的股價交易價格低於其帳面值的 25%。

在上述的例句中，我們用 compared with 來比較 Morgan Stanley 和 Goldman Sachs 的股價交易價格，同時配合百分比的數字，25% below……30% above，來做說明。

7-2 練習

▶ 找出下列句子中的增減比率。

1. Walmart, the world's biggest chain store, acquires 51% stake in Massmart, a South African retailing group, for $2.5 billion, which is 20% higher than Massmart's market value.

2. America's Retail Federation reported that 200 million shoppers bought goods either online or in store during the four-day thanksgiving period which sales reached to $45 billion in 2010 from $40 billion in 2009.

3. North Korea, which economic growth declined by 20% from 2000 to 2010, bombed on South Korea's island called Yeonpyeong and killed four people on November 23rd, 2010.

4. Mexico, a drug-ridden country, reported that 10,000 people had been killed in drug-related crime in 2010, compared with 80,000 in 2009.

5. President Obama's approval rating reached to 25%, an 80% decline since he took over the Oval Office after the Republican's landslide victory on mid-term election 2010.

6. California's budget was finally approved after 100 days of delay, and the budget remained $26 billion or about 20% of spending in deficit for 2011-2012.

7. Although the total cost of studying an four-year, in-state public college has nearly doubled to $20,000 between 2010s, the total benefits that with it are considerably huge.

8. Kim Jon-il in his early years as dictator-in-waiting had increased the country's military spending by 50% to $20 billion, 10% of GDP, from 1960 to 1990.

9. Although General Motors (GM) has successfully issued 20 million shares to raise $10 billion to pay back the bailout money, its share is still trading at 10% below its book value, compared with 20% above for Ford yesterday.

10. Business-sector productivity has impressively grown at annualized

rate of 5%, but labour costs have fallen by 2% at the same time. Business profit V-shape turnaround is at the expense of employee's wage L-shape.

7-2 解答

1. *20%*
   中譯：全球最大的量販連鎖店威瑪百貨以高於市場價值 20% 的價格，用 25 億美元取得南非零售集團 Massmart 51% 的股權。

2. *$45 billion in 2010 from $40 billion in 2009*
   中譯：美國零售聯合會報導指出在 4 天感恩節期間，有 2 億美國人透過網路或入店方式購物，消費金額從 2009 年的 400 億美元增加到 2010 年的 450 億美元。

3. *20% from 2000 to 2010*
   中譯：在 2000 年到 2010 年期間經濟成長率衰退 20% 的北韓，在 2010 年 11 月 23 日轟炸南韓延平島，造成 4 人死亡。

4. *100,000 people, 80,000*
   中譯：被毒品纏身的墨西哥國家，在 2009 年有 80,000 人死於和毒品相關的犯罪，比較下在 2010 年有 100,000 人死於該項目下。

5. *25%, an 80% decline*
   中譯：歐巴馬總統的施政滿意度於共和黨在 2010 年期中選舉取得壓倒性勝利之後，降到 25%，和他當初入主橢圓辦公室時比較起來下跌了80%。

6. *20%*
   中譯：在經過 100 天的延遲之後，加州的預算終於通過了，但是該預算在 2011-2012 年度中仍然有 260 億美元或是 20% 的預算金額是赤字。

7. *doubled to $20,000*
   中譯：雖然在就讀本州四年制公立大學的學雜費於 2010 年代期間幾

乎加倍,增加到 20,000 美元,但是跟隨而來的好處卻遠超過這些成本。

8. *50% to $20 billion, 10% of GDP*

　中譯:金正日早年還沒成為獨裁者之前,在 1960 年和 1990 年期間增加北韓軍事費用支出 50%,大約 200 億美元,相當於國內生產毛額的 10%。

9. *10% below, 20% above*

　中譯:雖然通用汽車成功的發行 2,000 萬股股票,募集 100 億美元來償還紓困貸款,通用汽車的股價成交價格在昨天仍然低於其帳面值 10%,而福特汽車的成交價格高於其帳面值 20%。

10. *annualized rate of 5%, 2%*

　中譯:企業部門的生產力以驚人的年化成長率 5% 增加,但是同一時間內勞動成本卻下降 2%,企業利潤的 V 型反轉卻使勞工工資付出慘痛的代價。

■7.3 金額寫法和讀法

在《經濟學人》的商業文章中常出現以企業營業額或獲利的報導，這些經營數據大都以當地的貨幣為計價單位，例如報導日本企業的獲利數據時以日圓為單位（￥），但是畢竟在西方國家是以美元為計價單位，再加上美元在國際貿易的重要地位，為了讓讀者了解以美元為計價單位的獲利數據，免除匯率換算的麻煩，因此在《經濟學人》文章中的金額都在當地貨幣計價單位數據之後，以括號方式加註以美元為計價單位的價值，讓讀者了解金額大小，我們來看下面的例句：

European policymakers agreed a €110 billion ($146 billion) bailout package for Greece in May.

五月時歐洲眾領導人同意支付 1,100 億歐元（1,460 億美元）的紓困方案給希臘。

在上述的例句中，紓困方案是 110 billion 歐元，以歐元對美元匯率（1:1.32）來計算的話，就是 146 billion 美元，讀者不用去查匯率，就知道歐元和美元的匯率為 1:1.32，增加文章閱讀的方便性，我們再看下面的例句：

Mitsubishi Group, Japan's multinational firm, reported its third quarter consolidated earnings ￥600 billion ($6.8 billion), a 20% increase compared with second quarter result.

日本多國籍企業三菱集團申報第三季的合併淨利為 6,000 億日圓（68 億美元），比第二季增加了 20%。

在上述的例句中，日本三菱集團的第三季淨利為 600 billion 日圓換算為 6.8 billion 美元，讀者可知美元和日圓的匯率為 1:88。國際間常用的貨幣單位如表 7-1 所示。

表7-1　國際常用貨幣單位

中文	英文	符號	代碼
美元	U.S. Dollar	$	USD
日圓	Japanese Yen	￥	JPY
英鎊	British Pound (The Pound Sterling)	£	GBP
歐元	The Euro	€	EUR

在文章中書寫這些金額是以 $10 billion 的方式來書寫，但是在大聲朗讀時卻是不同的排列方式，我們來看下面的例句：

Ford's first quarter earnings reached $2 billion.

福特汽車第一季獲利為 20 億美元。

朗讀的念法為：

Ford's first quarter earings reached 2 billion United States dollars.

在上述的文章中 $2 billion 的念法為：

2 billion United States dollars

我們再看下面的例句：

Marc Simoncini had set up Jaina Capital, a €100 million ($130 million) fund to invest four or five French start-ups over the next three years.

馬可‧希蒙希尼已成立 1 億歐元的珍納資本基金，未來三年內將投資四到五家法國的新創事業。

在上述的例句中，a €100 million ($130 million) fund 用朗讀的話，就必須念為 a hundred million euro dollars or one hundred thirty million United States dollars fund，其中（ ）我們念為 or。

7-3 練習

▶ 請將下列例句中的貨幣單位和金額，以朗讀方式大聲念出來。

1. Pepsi, the world's second largest soft drink maker, announced second quarter earings of $2 billion which one-sixth of the total was coming from the oversea market.

2. The European Central Bank (ECB) bought €2 billion ($2.6 billion) of euro-denominated bonds in the week ending December 10th.

3. Nomura Group, a Japanese securities firm, is reported to pay ¥200 billion ($2.2 billion) to acquire Lehman Brothers, the fallen wealth management of Wall Street titan.

4. Qatar, the Middle East oil and natural gas export country, will host the football World Cup in 2022, and it plans to spend $20 billion to build 12 climate-controlled stadiums to host the event.

5. Thousands of British students took to the streets yesterday to protest the skyrocketing tuition fee which was totally £20,000 ($30,000) for a four-year public university.

《經濟學人》這樣讀就對了

7-3 解答

1. *two billion United States dollars*
   中譯：全球第二大的飲料製造廠百事可樂宣布第二季獲利 20 億美元，其中六分之一的獲利來自海外市場。

2. *two billion euro dollars or two point six billion United States dollars*
   中譯：歐洲中央銀行在 12 月 10 日前買入 20 億歐元（26 億美元），以歐元計價的債券。

3. *two hundred billion Japanes yen or two point two billion United States dollars*
   中譯：據報導日本的證券公司野村集團將出資 2,000 億日圓（22 億美元），收購華爾街倒閉的巨人雷曼兄弟的財富管理部門。

4. *twenty billion United States dollars*
   中譯：中東產油和天然氣的國家卡達將主辦 2022 年世界杯足球賽，卡達將花費 200 億美元興建 12 座可調控氣候的體育場來主辦這項賽事。

5. *twenty thousand sterling or thirty thousand United States dollar*
   中譯：數以千計的英國學生昨天走上街頭抗議高漲的學雜費，四年制的公立大學學雜費支出總共 2 萬元英鎊（3 萬美元）。

第七章 綜合練習

▶ 請將下列文章中的數據找出來，並針對金額部分以朗讀方式書寫出來。

When Alan Mulally, a Boeing veteran, arrived at Ford Motors, he organized a weekly meeting of senior managers and asked them how thing was forecasted for the next ten years. Everybody said everything was going as planned. "We are forecasting $20 billion loss and no one has any problem," said Mr. Mulally. Mr. Mulally took the dramatic actions by cutting costs, improving product quality, lowering debt and increasing marketing campaign.

Five years on, Ford is reporting record breaking profit of $3 billion in 2010 fiscal year, twice as much as a year before and the sixth quarterly surplus in a row. One-third of the earnings is coming from the oversea market where China has seen a 30% increase, compared with last year figure. Although Chrysler, the smallest car maker of the Big Three, and General Motors (GM) are still in the government's hand at the result of the $300 billion bailout plan, Ford has taken the market share, which increases to 20% of the North America market, at the expense of the two. "Today we built Ford without your tax money," says one of its employees.

Mr. Mulally is demanding its floor managers to cut production costs to meet the challenge of Japan's transplant factories in America. Eight out of ten of Ford's platforms are used in its global factories. Ford's design team has come out "A World Car" that can be sold in every market without major modification to achieve economies of scale. The result: a brand new Fiesta. Ford expects to sale more than 2 million of them globally.

▌第七章 綜合練習解答 ▌

▶ 下列文章中的數據已用下標線方式標示出來。

When Alan Mulally, a Boeing veteran, arrived at Ford Motors, he organized a weekly meeting of senior managers and asked them how thing was forecasted for the next ten years. Everybody said everything was going as planned. "We are forecasting $20 billion loss and no one has any problem," said Mr. Mulally. Mr. Mulally took the dramatic actions by cutting costs, improving product quality, lowering debt and increasing marketing campaign.

Five years on, Ford is reporting record breaking profit of $3 billion in 2010 fiscal year, twice as much as a year before and the sixth quarterly surplus in a row. One-third of the earnings is coming from the oversea market where China has seen a 30% increase, compared with last year figure. Although Chrysler, the smallest car maker of the Big Three, and General Motors (GM) are still in the government's hand at the result of the $300 billion bail-out plan, Ford has taken the market share, which increases to 20% of the North America market, at the expense of the two. "Today we built Ford without your tax money," says one of its employees.

Mr. Mulally is demanding its floor managers to cut production costs to meet the challenge of Japan's transplant factories in America. Eight out of ten of Ford's platforms are used in its global factories. Ford's design team has come out "A World Car" that can be sold in every market without major modification to achieve economies of scale. The result: a brand new Fiesta. Ford expects to sale more than 2 million of them globally.

▶ 金額以朗讀方式書寫出來:

$20 billion twenty billion United States dollars

$3 billion three billion United States dollars

$300 billion three hundred billion United States dollars

第七章 單 字

- ★a poll 一項民調
- ★conduct 主導、執行
- ★a research firm 研究機構
- ★residents 居民
- ★Canada 加拿大
- ★Mexico 墨西哥
- ★the United Kingdom 英國
- ★two-thirds 三分之二
- ★approve 允許、核准
- ★full-body 全身
- ★X-Ray X光
- ★airport scanner 機場掃描器
- ★CBS News 哥倫比亞新聞
- ★Gallup 蓋洛普民調公司
- ★Wall Street
  華爾街（美國金融業）
- ★Main Street
  市區鬧街（一般民眾）
- ★a search engine 搜尋引擎
- ★handle 處理
- ★two out of three 三分之二
- ★account 總量
- ★billion 10億
- ★a given day 每一天
- ★Yukio Hotoyama 鳩山由紀夫
- ★in a row 排列成一列的
- ★resignation 辭職
- ★PMs 首相（prime ministers的縮寫）
- ★Taro Aso 麻生太郎
- ★Yasuo Fukuda 福田康夫
- ★Shinzo Abe 安倍晉三
- ★Yoshiro Mori 森喜郎
- ★heir 後代、繼承人
- ★political dynasty 政治家族
- ★leadership 領導特質
- ★the poverty line 貧窮線
- ★income 收入
- ★per day per head 每人每天
- ★enrollment 登記、入學
- ★housing bust 房地產崩盤
- ★credit crisis 信用危機
- ★executive 主管
- ★violate 違反
- ★human rights 人權
- ★impose 實施
- ★censorship 審查
- ★snow-capped mountain
  白雪覆蓋的山
- ★resort 渡假村
- ★Switzerland 瑞士
- ★delegent 代表
- ★think 認為
- ★responsibility 責任
- ★carbon dioxide 二氧化碳
- ★emission 排放
- ★green house effect 溫室效應
- ★growth 成長

★in term of 以～來計算

★sales revenue 營業收入

★slow 停滯、緩慢

★indicate 指示、表示

★glorous day 輝煌的日子

★onslaught 攻擊、猛攻

★internet ads 網路廣告

★fourth quarter 第四季

★beat 打敗

★analyst 分析師

★expectation 期待、期望

★Android 手機作業系統

★account 占有

★archrival 主要競爭對手

★dominate 主宰

★market share 市場占有率

★below 在～之下

★consumer spending 消費者支出

★decade 10年

★European 歐洲人

★easy money 多餘的資金

★budget deficit 預算赤字

★hight unemployment 高失業

★unsustainable
　不穩定的、無法支撐的

★social welfare 社會福利

★cause 原因

★misery 痛苦、苦楚

★the euro zone 歐元區

★publish 出版、發表

★survey 調查

★the West 西方國家

★carbon-based economies
　以碳為基礎的經濟

★alternative-energy-based
　economies
　替代能源為基礎的經濟

★Fitch 惠譽

★a rating agency 信用評等機構

★downgrade 調降

★long-term debt 長期負債

★reflect 反應

★earnings 淨利

★decline 下降

★Ireland 愛爾蘭

★Celtic tiger
　凱爾特之虎（愛爾蘭之虎）

★used to 習慣於、常用做

★Asian tigers 亞洲小龍

★achieve 達成

★export-led 出口帶動

★annual 每年、年化的

★average 平均

★the Fed (Federal Reserve Bank)
　聯邦儲備銀行

★Quantitative Easing 2.0 (QE2.0)
　第二次量化寬鬆政策

★loose 寬鬆的

★monetary policy 貨幣政策

★create 創造

★mean 表示、代表

★Morgan Stanley 摩根史坦利

★share 股票
★trade 交易
★below 之下、低於
★book value 帳面值
★compared with 比較
★above 之上、高於
★Goldman Sachs 高盛
★acquire 取得
★stake 股份
★retailing group 零售集團
★market value 市場價值
★federation 聯合會
★shopper 消費者
★thanksgiving period
　感恩節期間
★bomb 轟炸
★Mexico 墨西哥
★drug-ridden 毒品纏身的
★drug-related 毒品相關的
★approval rating 滿意度
★the Oval Office 橢圓辦公室
★landslide victory 壓倒性勝利
★double 加倍
★benefit 利益、好處
★considerably 考慮
★Kim Jong-il 金正日
★dictator-in-waiting
　成為獨裁者之前
★military spending 軍事費用支出
★business-sector 企業部門
★productivity 生產力

★impressively 驚訝的
★annualized 年化的
★labour costs 勞動成本
★V-shape V型
★turnaround 反轉
★at the expense 付出代價
★employee 勞工、雇員
★wage 工資
★L-shape L型
★policymaker
　領導人、政策制定者
★package 方案
★Greece 希臘
★multinational firm 多國籍企業
★consolidated 合併
★earings 獲利、淨利
★¥ 日圓
★start-ups 新成立之企業
★Pepsi 百事可樂
★oversea market 海外市場
★The European Central Bank
　(ECB) 歐洲中央銀行
★euro-denominated 歐元計價
★Nomura Group 野村證券集團
★securities firm 證券公司
★acquire 取得、購入
★wealth management 財富管理
★Lehman Brothers 雷曼兄弟
★titan 巨人
★oil 原油

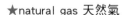

★natural gas 天然氣

★host 主辦

★football World Cup 世界杯足球賽

★climate-controlled 氣候監控的

★stadium 體育場

★protest 抗議、示威

★skyrocketing 暴漲的

★tuition fee 學雜費

★totally 總共

★Boeing 波音公司

★veteran 老兵、老鳥

★organize 主辦、安排

★weekly 每週的

★senior 資深的

★forecast 預估、計畫

★loss 損失

★dramatic 重大的

★marketing 行銷

★campaign 活動

★record breaking 破紀錄的

★fiscal year 財政年度

★Chrysler 克萊斯勒

★the North America Market 北美市場

★tax money 租稅金額

★floor manager 工廠領班、經理

★meet 達到

★challenge 挑戰

★transplant factory 跨廠化工廠

★platform 底盤

★modification 修改

★economies of scale 規模經濟

★Fiesta 嘉年華

★expect 期待

★globally 全球化的

第八章 圖表的閱讀

導論

　　《經濟學人》在每期週刊的最後，都會呈現過去一週內各國經濟和金融市場的各種數據變化，作為讀者查閱或股市投資的參考，或是將這些資料集結成冊，作為《經濟學人》姐妹刊 *Economist Intelligence Unit* 的出版資料，提供學術研究機構或全球圖書館的查閱資料。一般來說，《經濟學人》的經濟和金融統計指數資料基本上可分為三大類，分別是(1)產出、物價指數和失業率；(2)貿易、匯率、預算和利率，和(3)股價指數。

■8.1 產出、物價指數和失業率

本表主要是用來衡量一國在一定期間內的總體經濟表現，分別為國內生產毛額變動率（Gross Domestic Product, GDP）、最近一期的工業產出（Industrial Production Latest）、消費者物價指數年增率（Consumer Prices）和失業率（Unemployment），我們以表8-1來加以說明。

在表頭首先註明此表的名稱（Table Output, prices, and job），如果是圖的話就用 Figure，表的話就用 Table，同時說明此表的計算單位為%（Unit: %），而後在縱座標為各國的名稱，雖然全世界有將近200個國家，但是《經濟學人》還是只列出象徵性的國家，從排名第一項的美國（Untied States）到最後一項的南非（South Africa），而橫座標的第一項為國內生產毛額（Gross Domestic Product, GDP），而其下又分為四項：②最新數據（Latest）分別為第三季的＋3.2（＋3.2 Q3）、③季數據（和上一季比較的變動率）（QTR*）為＋2.5（＋2.5）、④2010年預估數據（2010**）為＋2.8（＋2.8），和⑤2011年預估數據（2011**）為＋2.6（＋2.6），其中 GDP 的數據也就是一般報章雜誌所稱的經濟成長率（Economic Growth Rate）。例如美國 2011 年預估的 GDP 為＋2.6%，也就是其預估的經濟成長率為＋2.6%，而表 8-1 的另一項統計數據為最新工業產出數據（Industrial Production Latest），其數據為十月分的＋5.3（＋5.3 Oct），單獨列出工業產出數據的目的，在於 GDP 的計算包括商品和「勞務」的最佳生產價值，而勞務包括非生產性的服務業、金融業或旅遊業等，為了突顯工業生產事業的重要性，才會單獨列出「最新工業產出數據（Industrial Production, Latest）」，而第 7 項為衡量通貨膨脹率高低的消費者物價指數（Consumer Prices），其中又分為三項分別為⑧最新數據（Latest），為10 月分的＋1.2（＋1.2 Oct）、⑨一年前數據（Years ago）為－0.2（－0.2）和⑩ 2010 預估數據（2010**）為＋1.6（＋1.6），值得注意的是消費者物價指數是年化的數據，例如第⑧項最新數據為 10 月分的＋1.2，也就是將10 月分的月數據轉化為年化數據得到的＋1.2。

而第 11 項為依據各國定義所統計出來的失業率（Unemployment Rate），美國 11 月分的失業率為（9.8 Nov），如果將相同月分的物價指數和失業率加總起來，便成為一般經濟學家所稱的痛苦指數（Misery Index），痛苦指數愈高，代表一般民眾所面臨的經濟壓力愈大。從表 8-1 中，可看出各國最新的總體經濟表現。

表 8-1 產出、物價指數和失業率 (Table 8-1 Output, Prices, and Jobs)

unit:%

	1. Gross Domestic Product(GDP)/國內生產毛額				6 Industrial Production Latest/最新工業產出數據	7 Consumer prices/消費者物價指數			11 Unemployment Rate/失業率***
	2 Latest/最新數據	3 QTR*/季數據*	4 2010**/2010年預估數據**	5 2011**/2011年預估數據**		8 Latest/最新數據	9 Years ago/一年前數據	10 2010**/2010預估數據**	
美國 United States	+3.2	+2.5	+2.8	+2.6	+5.3 Oct	+1.2 Oct	−0.2	+1.6	9.8 Nov
日本 Japan									
中國 China									
英國 Britain									
加拿大 Canada									
歐元區 Euro area									
奧地利 Austria									
比利時 Belgium									
法國 France									
德國 Germany									
希臘 Greece									
義大利 Italy									
荷蘭 Netherlands									
西班牙 Spain									
捷克 Czech Republic									
丹麥 Denmark									
匈牙利 Hungary									
挪威 Norway									
波蘭 Poland									
俄羅斯 Russia									
瑞典 Sweden									
瑞士 Switzerland									
土耳其 Turkey									
澳洲 Australia									
香港 Hong Kong									
印度 India									
印尼 Indonesia									
馬來西亞 Malaysia									
巴基斯坦 Pakistan									
新加坡 Singapore									
南韓 South Korea									
臺灣 Taiwan									
泰國 Thailand									
阿根廷 Argentina									
巴西 Brazil									
智利 Chile									
哥倫比亞 Colombia									
墨西哥 Mexico									
委內瑞拉 Venezuela									
埃及 Egypt									
以色列 Israel									
沙烏地阿拉伯 Saudi Arabia									
南非 South Africa									

* 和上一季比較之變動/年 %　　** 預估值　　*** 依各國定義

■8.2 貿易、匯率、預算和利率

　　而《經濟學人》的第二張統計表為針對各國貿易順差（逆差）、外匯匯率、政府預算和利率的統計表，如表 8-2 所示。在表 8-2 中的①項目為以商品貿易為主，單位為 10 億美元的最近 12 個月的貿易順差（逆差）金額（Trade balance lastest 12 month, $bn），日本的數據統計到 9 月分的 $919 億美元（91.9 Sep），一國之出口金額扣除進口金額之後若為正數，則一國享有貿易順差（trade surplus），若上述數據為負數，則一國享有貿易逆差（trade deficit），第②項目為針對一國資金進出所做統計的國際收支平衡表（Balance of Payment）中的經常帳餘額統計（Current-account balance），其中以金額來統計的為第③項單位為 10 億美元最近 12 個月的金額（latest 12 month, $bn）。日本統計到 10 月分為 $1,920 億美元（＋190.2 Oct），由於各國的經濟實力不均，為了求得各國均等的比較基礎，另以各國 GDP 為分母的統計數據，即為第④項的占 2010 年 GDP 的百分比（% of GDP 2010**），其中日本為＋3.4（＋3.4），以 GDP 做分母的經常帳餘額做比較，才可以看出各國經濟實力的強弱。第⑤項為各國貨幣對美元的匯率（Currency unit, per$），分別為第⑥項最新的匯率（Dec 8th），12 月 8 日美元對日圓的匯率為 84.3（84.3），而第⑦項為一年前的匯率（year ago），美元對日圓的匯率為 87.9（87.9），由此可得知過去一年當中美元對日圓貶值（depreciation），相反的為升值（appreciation）。而第⑧項為衡量政府預算赤字（盈餘）的指標：政府預算赤字（盈餘）占 2010 GDP 百分比（Budget balance % of GDP 2010）日本為－7.4（－7.4），代表日本政府預算赤字占 GDP 的比率為 7.4，如果一國政府收入大於支出則享有預算盈餘（budget surplus），相反的政府收入小於支出的話則一國享有預算赤字（budget deficit），第⑨項為一國之利率（Interest rates, %）分別為第⑩項的最新的 3 個月短期利率（3-month, latest），日本為 0.17，而第⑪項為代表長期利率的最新 10 年期政府公債利率（10-year gov't bonds, latest），日本為 1.21（1.21）。從以上這些數據的變動，可看出一國對外貿易和金額活動的高低之分，透過閱讀表 8-1 和表 8-2 這些金融和經濟數據，讀者對一國之經濟發展能有初步的了解。

表 8-2 貿易金額、外匯匯率、政府預算和利率(Table 8-2 Trade, Exchange Rates, Budget Balance, and Interest Rate)

	1 Trade balance* lastest 12 months, $bn / 最近12個月的貿易順差(逆差)的金額 單位:10 億美元	2 Current-account balance/經常帳餘額		5 Currency unit, per$/對$美元匯率			8 Budget balance % of GDP 2010** / 政府預算赤字(盈餘)占2010GDP百分比	9 Interest rates, %/利率, %	
		3 Latest 12 months, $bn /最近12個月的金額 單位:10 億美元	4 % of GDP 2010** / 占2010GDP的百分比	6 Dec 8th / 12月8日匯率	7 Year ago / 一年前匯率			10 3-month latest / 最新3個月月期利率	11 10-year gov't bonds, latest / 最新10年期政府公債利率
美國 United States									
日本 Japan	+91.9 Sep	+190.2 Oct	+3.4	84.3	87.9		-7.4	0.17	1.21
中國 China									
英國 Britain									
加拿大 Canada									
歐元區 Euro area									
奧地利 Austria									
比利時 Belgium									
法國 France									
德國 Germany									
希臘 Greece									
義大利 Italy									
荷蘭 Netherlands									
西班牙 Spain									
捷克 Czech Republic									
丹麥 Denmark									
匈牙利 Hungary									
挪威 Norway									
波蘭 Poland									
俄羅斯 Russia									
瑞典 Sweden									
瑞士 Switzerland									

表 8-2 貿易金額、外匯匯率、政府預算和利率(Table 8-2 Trade, Exchange Rates, Budget Balance, and Interest Rate)

| | 1 Trade balance* lastest 12 months, $bn / 最近12個月的貿易順差逆差金額 單位:10 億美元 | 2 Current-account balance/經常帳餘額 | | 5 Currency unit, per$/對$美元匯率 | | 8 Budget balance % of GDP 2010** / 政府預算赤字(盈餘)占2010GDP百分比 | 9 Interest rates, % / 利率, % | |
		3 Latest 12 months, $bn /最近12個月的金額單位:10 億美元	4 % of GDP 2010** / 占2010GDP的百分比	6 Dec 8th / 12月8日匯率	7 Year ago / 一年前匯率		10 3-month latest / 最新3個月期利率	11 10-year gov't bonds, latest / 最新10年期政府公債利率
土耳其 Turkey								
澳洲 Australia								
香港 Hong Kong								
印度 India								
印尼 Indonesia								
馬來西亞 Malaysia								
巴基斯坦 Pakistan								
新加坡 Singapore								
南韓 South Korea								
臺灣 Taiwan								
泰國 Thailand								
阿根廷 Argentina								
巴西 Brazil								
智利 Chile								
哥倫比亞 Colombia								
墨西哥 Mexico								
委內瑞拉 Venezuela								
埃及 Egypt								
以色列 Israel								
沙烏地阿拉伯 Saudi Arabia								
南非 South Africa								

*商品貿易為主　** 預估值

■8.3 股價指數

　　《經濟學人》所提供的第三種財經統計數據，為全球主要股市的指標性股價指數數據，總共有 59 個。有單一國家的股價指數，從 1 到 48；也有代表區域性經濟發展的股價指數，從 49 到 52；也有代表債券投資的指數，從 53 到 54；也有避險基金指數 55，代表美國股市變動風險高低的指數 56，衍生性金融商品指數，從 57 到 58，更有代表綠色產業的歐盟碳交易指數 59。例如美國道瓊工業指數在 12 月 8 日的收盤指數為 11,372.50（第 1 項的數據，11,372.50），而第 2 項的變動百分比又分為三小項，分別為第 3 項的一週變動百分比為＋1.0（＋1.0），如果以 2009 年 12 月 31 日為基期的話，則從 2010 年 1 月 1 日到 2010 年 12 月 8 日的變動百分比為第 4 項的 ＋9.1（＋9.1）。如果以美元計價的話，則為第 5 項的 ＋9.1（9.1）。例如日本日經 225 指數在第 4 項的變動百分比為 －3.0（－3.0），但是在 2010 年期間日圓對美元升值，造成日本日經 225 指數在第 5 項以美元計價的變動百分比反而為 ＋7.2（＋7.2）。

　　表 8-3 的最大功用在於幫助投資人於投資海外基金時，無論是單一國家投資、地區性投資、或是全球投資時，對當地股價指數的變動有初步的了解，才能決定進退場的時機，同時也能讓重視指數型投資人能有投資指數的標的，例如喜歡投資歐元區的共同基金投資人，便能選擇第 11 項的歐元區道瓊指數作為投資標的。

　　表 8-3 的另一個功用為股市是一國經濟表現的櫥窗，更是一國未來經濟展望樂觀或悲觀的領先指標，從第 4 項中便可看出以去年股價指數為基期，今年以來股價指數變動率，如果是正數的話，代表投資人對該國（該地區）未來經濟展望充滿樂觀；如果是負數的話，代表投資人對該國（該地區）未來經濟展望充滿悲觀。

表 8-3 股價指數（Table 8-3 Markets）

	1 Index Dec 08th / 12月08日指數	2 % change on/變動百分比		
		3 One week / 一週	4 In local currency / 以當地貨幣計價 Dec 31st 2009/2009年12月31日	5 In $ terms / 以美元計價
1 美國道瓊工業指數 DJIA	11,372.50	+1.0	+9.1	+9.1
2 美國標普500指數 S&P 500	1,228.3	+1.8	+10.1	+10.1
3 美國那斯達克指數 NAS comp	2,609.2	+2.3	+15.0	+15.0
4 日本日經225指數 Nikkei 225	10,232.3	+2.4	-3.0	+7.2
5 日本東部指數 Topix				
6 中國 上海上證A股指數 SSEA				
7 中國 上海上證B股指數美元計價 SSEB, $ terms				
8 英國金融時報100指數 Britain FTSE100				
9 加拿大標普綜合指數 Canada S&P TSX				
10 歐元區 金融時報歐期100指數 Euro area FTSE Euro 100				
11 歐元區道瓊50指數 Euro area DJ STOXX 50				
12 奧地利指數 Austria ATX				
13 比利時指數 Belgium Biel 20				
14 法國證商公會指數 France CAC 40				
15 德國 DAX指數 Germany DAX				
16 希臘雅典綜合指數 Greece Athex Comp				
17 義大利指數 Italy FTSE/MIB				
18 荷蘭 AEX指數 Netherlands AEX				
19 西班牙馬德里指數 SpainMadrid SE				
20 捷克指數 Czech Republic PX				
21 丹麥指數 Denmark OMXCB				
22 匈牙利指數 Hungary BUX				
23 挪威指數 Norway OSEAX				
24 波蘭指數 Poland WIG				
25 俄羅斯指數美元計價 Russia RTS $ terms				
26 瑞典指數 Sweden OMXS30				
27 瑞士指數 Switzerland SMI				
28 土耳其指數 Turkey ISE				
29 澳洲 指數 Australia All Ord				
30 香港恒生指數 Hong Kong Hang Seng				

表 8-3 股價指數 (續) (Table 8-3 Markets)

	1 Index Dec 08th / 12月08日指數	2 % change on/變動百分比 Dec 31st 2009/2009年12月31日		
		3 One week /一週	4 In local currency / 以當地貨幣計價	5 In $ terms / 以美元計價
31 印度指數 IndiaBSE				
32 印尼雅加達指數 Indonesia JSX				
33 馬來西亞可倫坡指數 Malaysia KLSE				
34 巴基斯坦指數 Pakistan KSE				
35 新加坡海峽時報指數 Singapore STI				
36 南韓指數 South Korea KOSPI				
37 臺灣加權指數 Taiwan TWI				
38 泰國指數 Thailand SET				
39 阿根廷指數 Argentina MERV				
40 巴西指數 Brazil BVSP				
41 智利指數 Chile IGPA				
42 哥倫比亞指數 Colombia IGBC				
43 墨西哥指數 Mexico IPC				
44 委內瑞拉指數 Venezuela IBC				
45 埃及指數 Egypt Case 30				
46 以色列指數 Israel TA-100				
47 沙烏地阿拉伯指數 Saudi Arabia Tadwul				
48 南非指數 South Africa JSEAS				
49 歐盟金融時報300指數 Europe FTSEurofirst 300				
50 全球已開發國家摩根史坦利資本指數 World dev'd MSCI				
51 新興國家 摩根史坦利資本指數 Emerging markets MSCI				
52 全球投資摩根史坦利資本指數 World all MSCI				
53 花旗世界債券指數 World bonds Citigroup				
54 JP摩根新興國家債券價券指數 EMBI JPMorgan				
55 避險基金指數 Hedge funds HFRX				
56 美國股市變動(風險)指數 Volatility, US VIX				
57 歐洲信用違約交換指數 CDs Eur iTRAXX				
58 北美市場信用違約交換指數 CDs N Am CDX				
59 歐盟碳交易指數 Carbon trading EU ETS				

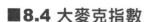

■8.4 大麥克指數

　　《經濟學人》最常被引用的數據，就是運用全球麥當勞餐廳所販賣的以當地貨幣計算的大麥克（Big Mac）價格，所計算出來一國貨幣對美元匯率是否高估或低估的指標，稱之為大麥克指數，如表 8-4 所示。

　　在第 1 項為大麥克漢堡的售價（Big Mac Prices），分別以該國貨幣計價的售價（第 2 項 In local currency）和以美元計價的售價（第 3 項 In dollars）。例如在第 2 項目下美國一個大麥克的售價為 3.54 美元，而在臺灣一個大麥克的售價為新臺幣 75 元，如果以美元對新臺幣的當日匯率計價的話，為臺灣大麥克的美元售價 2.23 美元，如果以臺灣大麥克的新臺幣售價 75 除以美國大麥克美元售價的話，便得到以貨幣購買力平價論（PPP）所得到的第 4 項美元對新臺幣匯率 21.2 NT／U$，而第 5 項為美元對該國貨幣的實際匯率，美元對新臺幣在 2009 年 2 月的匯率為 33.6 NT／U$，透過公式〔(21.2-33.6)／33.6〕便可得知新臺幣對美元匯率被低估 37%（第 6 項）。反言之，未來一年內新臺幣對美元應該升值 37%，或是未來一年內美元應該對新臺幣貶值 37%，透過簡單的大麥克指數，讀者便能得知未來該國貨幣對美元的匯率應該升值或貶值的趨勢了。

表 8-4 大麥克指數（Table 8-4 Big Mac Index）

	1 Big Mac Prices/大麥克售價		4 Implied PPP of the dollar / 用貨幣購買力平價理論所計算出的美元售價	5 Actual exchange rate, Jan 30th / 2009/2009年1月30日該國貨幣對美元實際匯率	6 Under(-)/over(+) valuation against the dollar, % / 該國貨幣對美元匯率被低估(-)被高估(+),百分比
	2 In local currency /以該國貨幣計價	3 In dollars /以美元計價			
美國 United States	$3.54	$3.54			
阿根廷 Argentina					
澳洲 Australia					
巴西 Brazil					
英國 Britain					
加拿大 Canada					
智利 Chile					
中國 China					
捷克 Czech Republic					
丹麥 Denmark					
埃及 Egypt					
歐元區 Euro area	€ 3.42	4.38	1.04	1.28	+24
香港 Hong Kong					
匈牙利 Hungary					
印尼 Indonesia					
以色列 Israel					
日本 Japan					
馬來西亞 Malaysia					
墨西哥 Mexico					
紐西蘭 New Zealand					
挪威 Norway					
秘魯 Peru					
菲律賓 Philippines					
波蘭 Poland					
俄羅斯 Russia					
沙烏地阿拉伯 Saudi Arabia					
新加坡 Singapore					
南非 South Africa					
南韓 South Korea					
瑞典 Sweden					
瑞士 Switzerland					
臺灣 Taiwan	NT$75.0	2.23*	21.2**	33.6	-37***
泰國 Thailand					
土耳其 Turkey					

計算方式說明　*(75/33.6)=2.23　　**(75/3.54)=21.2　　***((21.2-33.6)/33.6)= -37

第八章 單 字

★Figure 圖

★Table 表

★economic growth rate 經濟成長率

★unemployment rate 失業率

★misery index 痛苦指數

★trade surplus 貿易順差

★trade deficit 貿易逆差

★balance of payment
國際收支平衡表

★current-account balance
經常帳餘額

★depreciation 貶值

★appreciation 升值

★budget surplus 預算盈餘

★budget deficit 預算赤字

第九章 附加說明

導 論

　　在《經濟學人》的文章中，有時會用特殊的寫作方式——附加說明，來增加文章閱讀的可行性，這些附加說明的寫作方式將於本章說明之。

■9.1 照片說明

有時在文章中有介紹人物時，會附上一張照片，同時指出該人在照片中的位置（right, left, middle）來做說明，我們來看下面的例句：

Julian Assange (pictured above right), an Australian journalist and editor in chief of WikiLeaks, a whistle blower website, was released on bail by Britain's high court.

澳洲籍記者也是維基解密的主編傑利安・阿山吉（上圖右邊）被英國高等法院裁定交保。

在上述的例句中有附上圖片，同時為了讓讀者了解新聞事件當事人，作者特別指出當事人在照片中的位置，這種英語用法為 pictured above right（上圖右邊）。如果是下圖左邊的話就是 pictured below left，如果有多人要介紹的話，就用以上照片從右到左來說明 pictured above, right to left，我們來看下面的例句：

David Cameron, Nicolas Sarkozy and Angela Merkel (pictured above, right to left) were attending the NATO summit meeting.

大衛・卡麥隆、尼克萊・薩柯齊，和安傑利拉・梅克爾（上圖從右到左）參加北大西洋公約組織的高峰會。

在上述的例句中，照片中有三個人排成一列，所以我們用上圖從右到左來說明 pictured above, right to left。照片位置說明的英文用法，如表9-1所示。

表9-1	照片位置英語說明用法	
	英文	中文
1	pictured above right	上方照片右邊
2	pictured above left	上方照片左邊
3	pictured above, right to left	上方照片由右到左
4	pictured above, first row right to left	上方照片第一排從右到左
5	pictured above, second row right to left	上方照片第二排從右到左

■9.2 附圖說明

有時文章中有附圖的話,則用見附圖的方式(see chart╱see map)來加以表示,例句如下:

Japan's economic growth reached the lowest in decade (see chart).

日本經濟成長達到 10 年來的最低點(見附圖)。

在上述的例句句尾,我們用見附圖 see chart 來做正文的補充說明。

如果以眾多圖片排列方式來說明新聞事件的發生經過時,則可用從順時鐘方向左上圖開始 pictured clockwise from top left 的英文單字來說明。

我們來看下面的例句:

Thousands of Greek workers and students took to the streets yesterday in Athens to protest the government's welfare cut (pictured clockwise from top left).

數以千計的希臘勞工和學生昨天走上雅典街頭,抗議政府刪減福利支出(見上圖順時鐘方向從左上開始)。

在上述的例句中,我們在句尾用見上圖順時鐘方向從左上開始 pictured clockwise from top left 來提醒讀者閱讀圖片的順序,逆時鐘方向則用 counterclockwise 來代表,畢竟圖片的說明力遠大於文字(A picture is worth a thousand words),順時鐘和逆時鐘的英文用法說明如表 9-2 所示。

表9-2	順時鐘和逆時鐘英文用法說明	
	英文	中文
1	pictured clockwise from top left	順時鐘方向從上方左邊開始
2	pictured counterclockwise from top left	逆時鐘方向從上方左邊開始

■9.3 相關文章說明

在每期《經濟學人》的開頭都有本期重點文章的摘要說明，同時在摘要說明中加註相關文章在第幾頁，來導引讀者閱讀，此時就用參閱第幾頁（see pages ××-××）的文字說明，或下篇報導（see next story），我們來看例句：

Reforms in Russia can not take place without a shake-up of the country's corrupt bureaucracy system (see pages 28-30).

如果沒有大力整頓貪腐的官僚系統，俄羅斯的改革不可能發生（相關文章請參閱 P.28-30）。

在上述的例句中，我們用 see pages 28-30 來導引讀者在第 28-30 頁中，更加深入的閱讀有關俄羅斯所面臨的改革困境。

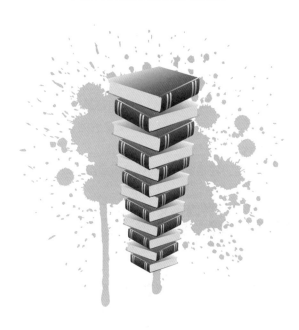

■9.4 附加說明

有時在《經濟學人》的文章中，也會用括號（ ）的方式來做補充說明，不過這種方式都是嘲諷的方式居多，我們來看下列例句：

The outlook of the world economy in 2011 depends on the performances of the big emerging markets, the euro area and the United States (Japan is still a heavy-weight economy, but the world doesn't expect the surprise yield).

2011 年全球經濟展望有待依賴新興國家、歐元區和美國等三大經濟體的表現（日本雖然是重量級的經濟體，但全球不期待日本有何驚奇的成長）。

在上述的例句中，我們用括號補充說明的方式，來嘲諷日本的經濟展望 Japan is still a heavy-weight economy, but the world doesn't expect the surprise yield。我們再看下面的例句：

Generous German and France subsidies of renewable energy benefit the solar power industry, but it disturbs the market order (and therefore costly).

德國和法國慷慨的對永續能源的補助，對太陽能產業大有幫助，但是這種補助打亂了市場秩序（因此代價很高）。

在上述的例句中，我們在句尾用括號說明的方式 and therefore costly 點出整個句子的重點，德國和法國再生能源政策的錯誤，達到畫龍點睛之效。

■9.5 《經濟學人》的文章架構

　　《經濟學人》整篇文章架構的寫作方法，在文章中的第一段就把整篇文章的事件背景、相關人物的發言意見和看法，做簡單的說明，讓讀者在讀完第一段的文章之後，就能對整篇文章故事的來龍去脈有初步的了解。第二段開始針對此一事件的每一關係人立場和意見，做詳細的說明。文章的最後一段，才針對此一事件的相反看法做呈現，表示正反二面的平衡報導，讓讀者有獨立思考此一事件的空間，我們來看下面的例子：

Everyone wants to talk about education reform

For many America's children the education system is often treated as a talk shop. (1) The White House, (2) state governments, (3) local governments and (4) teacher unions all have the rights to say about it. (1) The White house wants to increase the budget of No Child Left Behind plan (NCLB), first launched by President Bush. (2) State governments like Washington and Oregon want to impose mandatory state wide test for high school students. (3) Mark Lewis, the mayor of Orange County, California, for example, has used the state's education funds to support his pet project in the county. (4) Teacher unions, which have 500,000 members in the country, want to use the education reform to increase their pay.

(1) President Obama said that America has the best universities in the world but it's youngsters perform worst at several international math and art competitions. President Obama will --------

(2) Washington and Oregon are launching standard test programs to evaluate high school student performance before they can graduate from the school. Oregon is --------

(3) Many counties have used the state-supported funds in other state projects. Orange County, California, for example,

uses 15% of the annual education funds to support the local football clubs. Chicago was --------

(4) David Law, president of National Public School Teacher Union (NPSTU), called its members to boycott the pay for performance salary plan supported by President Obama. Mr. law --------

(5) Although America public school is a mess, many parents still believe that the federal government should stay away from the education reform. Parents have the final say about how their children should be taught. Even the world's best public school system, for example, Sweden and Demark, has its own problems.

在文章中的第一段，針對美國的教育制度改革，包括(1)The White House（白宮）；(2)state governments（州政府）；(3)local governments（地方政府）和(4)teacher union（教師工會），都有其立場和想要表達的重點。在第二段開始，針對教育改革的每一關係人立場和意見做詳細的說明、分段逐一陳述，在文章中分別以(1)、(2)、(3)和(4)段做說明，而在文章的最後一段才以(5)的方式，比較美國和其他國家的教改缺失做補充說明，呈現平衡式的報導，讓讀者針對美國教改問題有不同面向的思考模式。

第九章 單字

★Julian Assange
　傑利安・阿山吉
★pictured above right 上圖右邊
★journalist 記者
★editor in chief 主編
★WikiLeaks 維基解密
★whistle blower 檢舉人
★release 釋放
★bail 保釋
★high court 高等法院
★reform 改革
★shake-up 大力整頓
★corrupt 貪腐
★bureaucracy 官僚
★outlook 展望

★depend 依賴、依靠
★performances 表現
★heavy-weight 重量級
★yield 成長
★generous 慷慨的
★subsidy 補貼
★renewable energy 再生能源
★benefit 造福（受益）
★solar power 太陽能
★disturb 干擾、打亂
★market order 市場秩序
★therefore 因此
★costly 成本很高、代價很高
★clockwise 順時鐘方向
★counterclockwise 逆時鐘方向

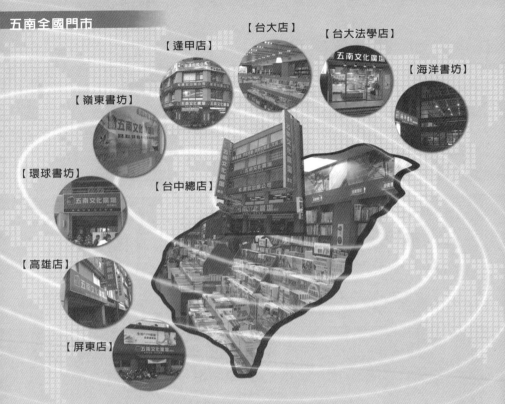

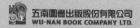

國家圖書館出版品預行編目資料

《經濟學人》這樣讀就對了／丁一著.
－－初版.－－臺北市：五南, 2012.08
　面；　公分.
ISBN 978-957-11-6612-4（平裝）
1.英語　2.讀本
805.18　　　　　　　　101004292

1067

《經濟學人》這樣讀就對了

作　　者 ― 丁　一
發 行 人 ― 楊榮川
總 編 輯 ― 王翠華
主　　編 ― 張毓芬
責任編輯 ― 侯家嵐
文字編輯 ― 陳俐君
封面設計 ― 盧盈良
排版設計 ― 張書易
出 版 者 ― 五南圖書出版股份有限公司
地　　址：106台北市大安區和平東路二段339號4樓
電　　話：(02)2705-5066　　傳　真：(02)2706-6100
網　　址：http://www.wunan.com.tw
電子郵件：wunan@wunan.com.tw
劃撥帳號：01068953
戶　　名：五南圖書出版股份有限公司
台中市駐區辦公室/台中市中區中山路6號
電　　話：(04)2223-0891　　傳　真：(04)2223-3549
高雄市駐區辦公室/高雄市新興區中山一路290號
電　　話：(07)2358-702　　傳　真：(07)2350-236
法律顧問　元貞聯合法律事務所　張澤平律師
出版日期　2012年8月初版一刷
定　　價　新臺幣250元